THE
GREENGAGE
SUMMER

THE GREENGAGE SUMMER

A NOVEL

RUMER GODDEN

OPEN ROAD

INTEGRATED MEDIA

NEW YORK

Copyright © 1979 by Rumer Godden

ISBN: 978-1-5040-6658-7

This edition published in 2021 by Open Road Integrated Media, Inc.
180 Maiden Lane
New York, NY 10038
www.openroadmedia.com

THE
GREENGAGE
SUMMER

CHAPTER I

On and off, all that hot French August, we made ourselves ill from eating the greengages. Joss and I felt guilty; we were still at the age when we thought being greedy was a childish fault and this gave our guilt a tinge of hopelessness because, up to then, we had believed that as we grew older our faults would disappear, and none of them did. Hester of course was quite unabashed; Will—though he was called Willmouse then—Willmouse and Vicky were too small to reach any but the lowest branches, but they found fruit fallen in the grass; we were all strictly forbidden to climb the trees.

The garden at Les Oeillets was divided into three; first the terrace and gravelled garden round the house; then, separated by a low box hedge, the wilderness with its statues and old paths; and, between the wilderness and the river, the orchard with its high walls. In the end wall a blue door led to the river bank.

The orchard seemed to us immense and perhaps it was, for there were seven alleys of greengage trees alone; between them, even in that blazing summer, dew lay all day in the long grass. The trees were old, twisted, covered in lichen and moss, but I shall never forget the fruit. In the hotel dining room Mauricette built it into marvellous pyramids on dessert plates laid with vine leaves. "Reines Claudes" she would say to teach us its name as she put our particular plate down, but we were too full to eat. In the orchard we had not even to pick the fruit, it fell off the trees into our hands.

The greengages had a pale blue bloom, especially in the shade, but in the sun the flesh showed amber through the clear green skin; if it were cracked the juice was doubly warm and sweet. Coming from the streets and small front gardens of Southstone, we had not been let loose in an orchard before; it was no wonder we ate too much.

"Summer sickness," said Mademoiselle Zizi.

"Indigestion," said Madame Corbet.

I do not know which it was but ever afterwards, in our family we called that the greengage summer.

"You are the one who should write this," I told Joss. "It happened chiefly to you." But Joss shut that out as she always shuts out things, or shuts them in so that no one can guess.

"You are the one who likes words," said Joss. "Besides"— and she paused—"it happened as much to you."

I did not answer that. I am grown up now—or almost grown up—"and we still can't get over it!" said Joss.

"Most people don't have . . . that . . . in thirty or forty years," I said in defence.

"Most people don't have it at all," said Joss.

If I stop what I am doing for a moment, or in any time when I am quiet, in those cracks in the night that have been with me ever since when I cannot sleep and thoughts seep in, I am back; I can smell the Les Oeillets smells of hot dust and cool plaster walls, of jasmine and box leaves in the sun, of dew in the long grass; the smell that filled house and garden of Monsieur Armand's cooking and the house's own smell of damp linen, or furniture polish, and always, a little, of drains. I can hear the sounds that seem to belong only to Les Oeillets: the patter of the poplar trees along the courtyard wall, of a tap running in the kitchen mixed with the sound of high French voices, of the thump of Rex's tail and another thump of someone washing clothes on the river bank; of barges puffing upstream and Mauricette's toneless singing—she always sang through her nose; of Toinette and Nicole's quick loud French as they talked to each other out of the upstair's windows; of the faint noise of the town and, near, the plop of a fish or of a greengage falling.

"But you were glad enough to come back," said Uncle William.

"We never came back," said Joss.

The odd thing was, when that time was over, we, Joss and I, were still sixteen and thirteen, the ages we had been when we arrived on the stifling hot evening at the beginning of August. We were Mother, Joss, I—Cecil—Hester, and the Littles, Willmouse and Vicky. It must have been nine o'clock.

"Why were you so late?" asked Mademoiselle Zizi. "There are plenty of trains in the day."

"We were waiting in the Gare de l'Est for Mother to get better."

"And she didn't get better," said Willmouse.

"And we had nothing to eat all day," said Vicky, "but some horrid sausage and bread."

"And the oranges we had with us," said Hester, who was always accurate, "twelve oranges. We ate them in the train."

Mademoiselle Zizi shuddered, and I burned to think that now she must know we were the kind of family that ate oranges in trains.

There had been no taxis at the station but, after a stress that I do not like to remember—the whole day had been like a bad dream—we found a porter who would take our suitcases on a handcart.

It was beginning to be dusk when our little procession left the station; men were coming back from fishing, women were talking in doorways and in their stiff gardens where gladioli and zinnias seemed to float, oddly coloured in the twilight, behind iron railings. "French people don't have gardens," Uncle William was to say, "they grow flowers." Children were playing in the streets; Willmouse and Vicky stared at them; I think they had thought they were the only children in the world kept up to this late hour.

All round us was the confusion of the strange town, strange houses, strange streets. The people stared at us too but we did not feel it; we did not feel anything; our bodies seemed not to belong to us but to be walking apart while we floated, as the flowers did, in the dusk. Perhaps we were too tired to feel.

The handcart bumped over cobbles that, even though we had not walked on cobbles before, we knew were unmistakably French. Mother gave a small moan each time the porter turned into another street. It seemed a long way and by the time we came to the hotel gates lamplight was showing in the houses and most of the doors were shut. At Les Oeillets every night at nine o'clock the dogs were let loose and the outer gates closed, leaving only a wicket gate unlocked; the handcart would not go through that and we had to wait—still apart from ourselves—while the porter rang the bell.

It clanged. There was a deep barking. We did not know Rex and Rita then but could tell it was a big dog's bark; two voices commanded it to stop, a woman's shrill, and a man's— or a boy's talking like a man; that was a good guess, for it was a large boy who appeared. He had on a white apron, we saw it glimmering towards us; his apron flapped, his shoes flapped too, and a lock of hair fell into his eyes as he bent forward to pull the bolt; he held the gate open to let us pass and we smelled his smell of sweat and cigarettes and . . . "Is it onions?" I whispered.

"Not onion, garlic," Hester whispered back. "Don't you remember the sausage in the Gare de l'Est?" He was dirty and untidy and he did not smile.

Then we went into the hotel and, "Good God! An orphan-age!" said Eliot.

Afterwards he apologized for that. "But you were all wearing grey flannel," he said and he asked, "Why were you wearing grey flannel?"

Hester looked at him. "Perhaps you haven't been in Eng-land for a long time," she said gently. "Those were our school clothes."

In England we—except Joss—had been proud of them. There are two sorts of families; for one a school uniform is a step down, the feeling of being like everybody else; for the other that feeling is an achievement, the uniform a bet-ter, more complete set of clothes than any worn before; we belonged to the second category and Willmouse's grey shorts and jacket, our St. Helena's coats and skirts and hats were our best clothes, the only ones suitable for travelling.

"Other girls have other clothes," Joss said often.

"Not when an Uncle William pays for them," said Mother.

Now Joss's eyes threw darts of hate at Eliot though he could not have been expected to know who she was. Our school hats were soup-plate shaped; Vicky in hers looked like a mushroom on two legs, but Joss's was small on her mass of dark hair and showed her forehead; she looked almost ugly in that hat, and the pleated skirt of her suit was too short.

Of course a great many things happened before Eliot said that about the orphanage; he did not even come in until later; but it is Eliot whom we remember of that first evening. He was its ace.

"When he came there was no more dreadfulness," said Hester, but I had to add, "Except *the* dreadfulness."

CHAPTER II

"What! Only two passports?" said Mademoiselle Zizi when I took ours to the office next morning.

"Joss, my sister, has hers, the rest of us are on my mother's." I hated to have to say that. The hotel boy who had let us in was listening—his name, we knew now, was Paul; he was scornfully polishing the brass grille and could squint down at the passports. His look said plainly that he would not go about with a mother.

I had fought about that passport. "Why should Joss have one and not I?"

"She is sixteen," said Mother, and added, "You forget how young you are."

Three years separated each of us children—Father's expeditions usually lasted three years—but Joss and I had always been the Big Ones, as Willmouse and Vicky were the Littles, with Hester in a no-man's-land between. JossandCecil, it had been one word though it had meant I had sometimes to be older than I conveniently could; now I was relegated to a no-man's-land myself. I could see it was inevitable—thirteen is not child, not woman, not . . . declared, I, thought, as Joss was now—but it hurt. The separate passport was a pubic confirmation of the status Joss had taken for herself; she had moved into it quite naturally, leaving me behind as she had moved from the bedroom we had always shared into one of her own. "There are things," said Mother, purposely vague though she knew I knew perfectly well what those things were, and she had let Joss change with Willmouse, moving him in to me.

Hester would have been a more natural companion, but she could not be separated from Vicky. "I have to sleep with my foot in her bed, you see," said Hester.

"Your foot *out*, in *her* bed?" I asked.

"Yes, or she won't go to sleep."

"But isn't it cold?"

"Sometimes." Hester added I was not to tell Mother. A great deal of the peace in our house was kept by Hester, but I was shocked. I spoke to Vicky. "But that is how I know she is there," said Vicky as if that justified it.

"But it's naughty."

"I don't mind being naughty," said Vicky.

A line might have been run through our family dividing it, with Hester, Vicky, and me on one side, Joss and Willmouse on the other. Our surname was Grey: I wished it had been Shelmerdine or de Courcy, ffrench with two small fs, or double-barrelled like Stuvesant-Knox, but it was, simply, Grey. "Better than Bullock," said Joss. We had not quite escaped that; Uncle William was a Bullock, William John Bullock, and Vicky, Hester, and I were as unmistakably Bullock as he, short, bluff, pink-faced, with eyes as blue as larkspurs.

It was not as bad for Hester and Vicky because the Bull-ocks made pretty children; Vicky, fair-haired, with firm pearly flesh, was enchanting and Hester, with her ringlets and rosiness, had kept her appeal; but in me, as in Uncle William, the plumpness had become a solid shortness, the fair hair was mouse, the rosy cheeks a fresh pinkness. No one ever looked as normal as Uncle William, and I wanted to look startling. Why could I not have been born to look like Joss, to be Joss? Joss and Willmouse were dark and slim with such an ivory skin that their lashes and hair looked darker. "Like Snow White," said Hester with the only trace of envy I ever heard in her. They were, too, delicately unusual; Willmouse had the peaked look of an elf while Joss's eyes had the almond shape that had given her her nickname. "Because Chinese people have slant eyes," said Joss.

"Are supposed to have them," Father had corrected her on one of his times at home. "Most of them have eyes as straight as anyone."

"They have them in paintings," said Joss, who knew all about painting. She and Willmouse were equally vain—and clever; Joss was a serious painter and Willmouse had what we called his "dressage." It was years before we found out that that had to do with horses not clothes. Willmouse's scrapbooks and workbox and the dolls that so distressed Uncle William—"Dolls! Gordon's ghost!"—were part of it; the books held a collection of fashion prints, designs, and patterns of stuffs; Willmouse needed his scissors and pins for draping his designs—"I don't *sew*," he said, "that will be done in my workrooms,"—while the dolls, his models, Miss Dawn and Dolores, were not dolls but artist's lay-figures carved in wood with articulated joints. They had been given to Joss by Uncle William to help her in her painting but to Mother's bewilderment she would not touch them, while Willmouse had annexed them. Mother could deal with us little Bullocks. Though we were often rude or obstinate, "That is normal," said Mother, but with Joss and Willmouse it was as if, in our quiet farmyard, she had hatched two cygnets and, "Everything I do is wrong," said poor Mother.

It seemed to be; for instance, when Joss complained that the art mistress at St. Helena's was no use, Mother enrolled Joss in a London correspondence art course, but that had led to difficulties. "Dear Mr. A . . ." Joss wrote in the second lesson to her far-off master, "I send you the design you asked for using a flower, St. John's Wort, and the drawing of the woman—my mother—but I am sorry I cannot find a naked man anywhere."

With Joss and Willmouse even the Grey in their names took on an elegance; Joanna Grey, William Grey, had a good sound while Cecil or Victoria Grey were nothing, though Hester Grey suited Hester.

It had never been fair but now, I thought, it was growing more unfair, for Joss had blossomed; that was what people said of young girls and I saw it was the right word; she was like a tree or a branch where every bud was breaking into flower.

She would not undress with me any more and I was glad because my pinkness was still distressingly straight up and down while she had a waist now, slim and so supple I could not help watching it, and curves that tapered to long slim legs, while her breasts had swelled. I know how soft these were and that they were tender, for once, out of curiosity, I had touched them and she had jumped and sworn at me. As Joss grew, she grew more irritable, with flashes of temper that were sometimes cruel; she was restless too, as if she were always excited, which was odd because her face was serene and withdrawn, almost secret, I thought, with only the palest pink flush on her cheeks to tell of the excitement inside. "Is Joss beautiful?" I asked with a pang.

"Just now," said Mother. "Just now."

I tried desperately to keep up with Joss. Cecil de Courcy, de Haviland, Cecil du Guesclin, Winnington-Withers . . . Winter. That was a beautiful name and I thought, I shall use it when I am a writer, or a nun; Cecil Winter, Sister Cecilia Winter, but I was not yet a writer, or a nun, nor did I know that I should ever be either. At the moment I was more like a chameleon, coloured by other people's business, and now I burned as I had burned about us eating oranges in the train, when I saw Mademoiselle Zizi's lips twitch as she read out our names from Mother's passport. There was barely room for us all in the space.

"You went chasing across France with that gaggle of children?" Uncle William said afterwards.

"We didn't chase," said Mother. "We went quite slowly by train." Sometimes Mother was no older than Hester and that passport with its single stamp, in spite of all the names, looked like a child's.

"Et votre pète?" asked Madame Corbet.

"Yes. Where is your father?" asked Mademoiselle Zizi.

"In Tibet," said Hester.

"Ti-*bet*?"

I should have done better without Hester, who could never learn to temper anything it was odd—and annoying—that I always wanted us not to be ordinary but, when we were a little extraordinary, I blushed.

"Juste ciel! What is he doing in Tibet?" asked Mademoiselle Zizi.

"Picking flowers," said Hester.

"Picking flowers!" Mademoiselle Zizi repeated it in French, and Paul gave a short guffaw which made me rap out what was almost a French sentence: "Il est botaniste." I added, in English, that he was on an expedition. "He usually is," said Hester.

Mademoiselle Zizi and Madame Corbet looked at one another. "Mon Dieu! Mon Dieu! Eh quoi?" said Madame Corbet.

They began to talk about us in French as if we were not there. "They have not been in France before," said Mademoiselle Zizi, looking at the passports.

"They have not been anywhere," said Madame Corbet.

"We have," I began hotly. "My sister Joss was born in India. Mother's old passport expired, that's all . . ." But they did not listen.

"And they don't speak French."

That was wounding because, up to that moment, I had believed that Joss and I, particularly I, spoke French very well. "You ought to," said Joss. "You learned enough." That was not kind, for learning French poetry was a punishment at St. Helena's.

"Never mind," whispered Hester. "Look how it has helped you, being bad." Certainly it was the only thing at which I ever beat Joss, and the hours I had spent over "Le temps a laissié son manteau/De vent, de froidure et de pluye," "Mignonne, allons voir si la rose," and the Verlaines I had grown to love, had stood me in good stead; I had been able to understand, all that nightmare day, what people had said, and really it was I, more than Joss, who had piloted us all here. I *did* speak French but, as if he knew what I was thinking, Paul sniffed and drew his finger across his nose and wiped it on the back of his trousers, which looked rude.

"We cannot be expected to look after them," Madame Corbet was saying.

"We can look after ourselves," I said with dignity. "We are not little children."

Mademoiselle Zizi picked up Joss's passport and then threw it down on the desk. "Sixteen," she said, "a child," and asked me in English, "Have you no relative, no one at all who could come?"

Before I could stop her Hester had answered. "Uncle William."

Uncle William was Mother's brother, ten years older than she— "though it might have been a hundred," said Joss. Most grown people are like icebergs, three-tenths showing, seven-tenths submerged—that is why a collision with one of them is unexpectedly hurtful—but Mother was like a child, transparently above-board and open—"to any scallywag," said Uncle William.

I sometimes wondered if he ranked Father as a scallywag, but he did not say it and Uncle William said most things. "If you had listened to me," was his favourite. I do not think Mother had listened to him when she married but, all the same, when she brought Joss back from India—babies cannot go on expeditions—he had met them and brought them to Southstone, "And Belmont Road," said Joss bitterly.

"How did we know enough to hate it," she asked afterwards, "when it was all we could remember?" We disliked and were ashamed of the ugly cheap little house with its pebbledash, its imitation Tudor gables and leaded windows. "Silly to cut glass up into all those bits," said Willmouse, but it was one of Uncle William's houses, he owned several in Southstone, and he kindly let us live in it. "He *is* so kind!" Mother said and sighed.

Uncle William spent money and time and effort on us children, "And words," said Hester, "heaps and heaps of words," while Father came only at long intervals and, when he did come, hardly lifted his eyes from his collections of ferns or orchids to look at his wife and children. I think he could scarcely tell the Littles apart, yet we loved him and longed for him to come home; we ran our legs off on his errands and were proud of belonging to him. "Oh well," said Hester, "I will look after Uncle William when he is old."

Did we need Uncle William? I could never make up my mind, just as I could never make out if Mother was very silly or very wise. Take her dealings with Willmouse. "He says he won't wear it," she had said, handing back his new school cap at his school.

"Then he must leave," said the headmaster.

Mother consulted with Willmouse and, "He would rather leave," said Mother and Willmouse left, until Uncle William heard.

"Why can't I go to a girl's school?" asked Willmouse. "They don't have caps and perhaps I could wear my muff."

"Gordon's ghost!" said Uncle William.

The muff was white fur lined with satin; Willmouse had bought it with the money Uncle William gave him for his fifth birthday.

"What did you buy, boy? A cricket bat? A train?"

"A muff," said Willmouse.

"Gordon's ghost!" said Uncle William. We never discovered who the ghost was but Willmouse often made Uncle William say things like "Gordon's ghost" and "The only boy amongst them and he isn't a boy!"

Willmouse was little then but I think we, ourselves, sometimes wished we had a proper boy. "He is Willmouse," said Mother. That was what she understood about him, about us all, even Joss, in our different ways. Perhaps if she had been left to deal with us alone there would not have been the discontent and rudeness.

I think now that the discontent was because we were never quite comfortable in Southstone and the rudeness came from the discontent; it was as if a pattern-mould were being pressed down on us into which we could not fit. For one thing we were much poorer than the people we knew, poor to be Uncle William's sister, nieces, and nephew; and we had this curiously absent father while other girls' fathers went to offices and caught trains and belonged to the Sussex Club. Mother too was not like other mothers, nor like a grown-up at all; she patently preferred being with Vicky or Willmouse or any of us to playing bridge, or organizing bazaars, or having coffee or luncheon or tea with the select Southstone ladies. When any of us—except Hester, who was at home anywhere—went out to tea in one of the big red-brick houses, with lawns and laurel bushes and meticulously gravelled driveways, we felt interlopers. We were odd, belonging and not belonging, and odd is an uncomfortable thing to be; we did not want to belong but were humiliated that we did not. I know now it was not good for us to live in Southstone. We should not have been as odd somewhere bigger, in London perhaps.

"In London," said Joss dreamily, "you can be anyone. You never know whom you are sitting next to. He might be a beggar or a duke."

"Or a thief," said Uncle William, who had decided views on London.

"Southstone—" I began.

"Is where you live," said Uncle William.

"It's all middle, middle, middle," I said in despair. It was. No beggars and no dukes. "Just middle."

"My dear child, that is the world."

"The world is not all middle," said Joss.

"Most of it is. Why should you be different?"

We could not think of any reason, yet we knew we were; every heartbeat told us that. "How shall we ever get out of Southstone?" I asked Joss in despair.

Then we were rude to Mother again and she took us to Vieux-Moutiers, Vieux-Moutiers and Les Oeillets.

I do not know what it was that drove her to it. Probably Joss and I had been more than usually difficult and unkind, for I had followed Joss in this new bullying of Mother, of being horrid to Hester and snapping at the Littles, of criticizing; I joined in from habit and from principle.

"Oh Mother! You are so slow."

"Do we have to have that *disgusting* old tea cosy?"

"*Must* you wear that hat?"

I think, at that time, she was only happy when she was with Willmouse and Vicky; she and Hester were too alive to know if they were happy together or not; it would have been like trying to know if one were happy in one's own skin.

"*Why* do you have to have a shopping bag?" Joss would say.

"To put the shopping in," said Mother, astonished.

"*Why* must Hester wear plimsolls in the street?"

"She is going on the beach."

It was on the beach that it happened.

We did not go away for the summer holidays—"or any holidays," said Joss discontentedly—but spent long days on the beach, picnicking. "Must we?" asked Joss.

"I thought you liked it," said Mother, but Joss shuddered.

Our picnics were even more family ones than most; we had baskets and bags bulging with bathing towels and Thermos flasks, and a dreadful aluminium food container, brought home by Father from India, that was always coming apart in the street. We had buckets and spades and shrimping nets, jerseys and paper bags. "Like a bank holiday," said Joss, "and must Hester talk to *everyone*? She's such a blatant child."

We had to wear what we called our scarecrows, old faded-out patched cottons. "I can't help it," said Mother. "I can't let your good clothes get covered with salt and oil."

"We haven't any good clothes," said Joss.

Mother was gentle but that day we went too far. I do not remember what we did, but she lost her temper. "You are abominably selfish," she said.

When she was angry she did not go white as Joss did; she went pink. "You never think of anyone but yourselves."

We stared. Whom else should we think of?

"Everyone tells me you are badly brought up and it's true."

"You brought us up," said Joss.

"It's true," repeated Mother.

"What are you going to do about it?" I asked as insolently as I could, and Hester stole a hand into hers.

"I shall do something.

"What?"

Mother took a deep breath. "I shall take you to the battle-fields of France."

"The *battlefields* of *France*!"

We were still speaking rudely but it was feeble, the last intermittent gunfire before surrender. "Why?"

"So that you can see what other people have given," said Mother, "given for your sakes; and what other people will do in sacrifice. Perhaps that will make you ashamed and make you think. And Saint Joan," said Mother, "Saint Joan at the stake. We shall stop wherever it was and see where she was burned."

"Oh Mother! Not in the middle of the summer holidays!"

"Holidays or not," said Mother, and shut her lips.

"Pooh! You haven't enough money," said Joss, but she sounded a little frightened.

"I shall use the legacy."

"The legacy is for college," said Joss.

"This is college," said Mother. "It is education. You need to learn . . . what I cannot teach you," said Mother, her voice quivering.

She did not ask Uncle William's advice. She went to Mr. Stillbotham.

Mr. Stillbotham was an elderly Theosophist who lived in Belmont Road and was the only person in it, as far as we knew, who travelled. Father, of course, could not be said to live in

Belmont Road. Mr. Stillbotham spent his winters in the South of France; we admired him for that and thought him distinguished with his silver hair, pince-nez, blue and white striped shirts, and bow ties. We also liked his manner to us, which was full of courtesy and admiration—particularly for Joss.

"Standing with reluctant feet
Where the brook and river meet,"

Mr. Stillbotham would say when he saw her. Altogether he seemed a suitable person to advise us, and we approved.

"You wish to visit your dead?" he asked when Mother told him about the battlefields. "They are not dead but liv—" but for the purposes of our visit Mother needed them dead and she cut him short. "Can you tell us of an hotel, not too expensive, and near the cemeteries?" she said.

"Les Oeillets at Vieux-Moutiers." That was the first time we heard its name. "You will find plenty of motors at the station."

Saint Joan had been burned, it seemed, at Rouen. "But you can break your journey there if you go by Newhaven-Dieppe, which will be cheaper," said Mr. Stillbotham, "or if you preferred it, you could spend the afternoon in Paris."

Spend the afternoon in Paris! Saint Joan had not the slightest chance after that. "I shall see the Louvre," said Joss. "'Mona Lisa.' The 'Winged Victory.'"

"I shall see the shops," said Willmouse and, as always when he was stirred, his face went white.

"Do you remember those strawberry tarts, little strawberries in syrup, that Father once brought back?" asked Vicky. "They came from Paris," she said reverently.

Hester and I, as usual, were far more ordinary; she would be happy buying postcards and taking snapshots with her Brownie camera, while I, the chameleon, would be with them all in turns. "Well, you enjoy it more in that way," said Mother. We were all equally excited.

"If you listen to me . . ." said Uncle William, but nobody listened.

"Very well," said Uncle William. "When you get into trouble don't ask me for help."

"We shall not need help," said Mother, dignified; but the day before we left she was bitten on the leg by a horsefly. "A little fly," said Hester, "to do all that!"

When Mother took down her stocking in the train from Dieppe, the leg was swollen and the skin looked purple, green, and blue. "Like a bruise," said Hester. "Did you bruise it? All over?" she finished uncertainly.

Mother shook her head. She fumbled with her handbag as if she could not control her hands and she shivered although she was hot.

"You are ill," said Joss accusingly, and Mother could not deny it.

It was altogether a disappointing as well as a dismaying day. From the train France did not look very different from England, it had the Constable, Peter Rabbit colours we had grown up with, and in Paris we did not see the Louvre, or the shops, or eat strawberry tarts. We did not buy a single postcard, or take a photograph; we waited in the waiting room for Mother to get well. The attendant in a dark blue overall with a black crochet shawl came and looked at us but we were too shy to speak to her. "Why didn't you go to Cook's? Lunn's?

The American Express? Any of them would have helped you."
Uncle William has asked us that often but Joss and I had then
only one idea: to get Mother, the Littles, Hester, ourselves, and
our suitcases to Vieux-Moutiers and Les Oeillets.

There was a train at seven. I remember I went to a food
wagon and bought rolls and sausage. I did not know what else
to buy and Joss would not go. "But you are the eldest," I said.

"You are the best at French," said Joss cruelly.

Like a herd we drew together and sniffed the sausage; we
had not smelled garlic before and we gave it to the attendant;
we ate the rolls.

I remember when Vicky touched Mother's leg, Mother
gave a little scream and quickly bit her lips. "Don't worry," she
said in a moment, "one is not sent anything one can't bear," but
she had to bite her lips again. I remember too that Willmouse
disappeared. "Il est parti voir les locos," said the attendant, but
there was a new *Vogue* on a kiosk and he had gone to look at
that, not at the engines.

I do not remember the train, only that Mr. Stillbotham had
been wrong and there were no taxis at the station. We had to
take a porter and a hand cart.

"But Mother can't walk," said Hester.

"She must." A terrible hardness had come upon us. We
took her by her arms. She moaned and stumbled, and Hester
wept. At last we came to the gates.

As we waited after the porter rang the bell, I moved away
from the others. I had had the sudden sharp sense of a garden, sharp because it cut me from them. Through the gates I
could see a courtyard with gravel round a square of grass in
front of the house. To the side, paths led away into the trees;

the light was almost gone now and trees showed dimly, grey-green along the wall, while the garden was black in the depth of the shadows. There was a steady light pattering sound—I did not know then that French sound of poplar leaves. A bird gave a sleepy call; an owl answered it, that strange night noise that I recognized though I had not heard it before.

I could smell a summer smell of cut grass and, near me, some flower scent that was heady and sweet; a white flower, I thought, jasmine or syringa. After the city and train my skin was cinder-dry and the air was gratefully cool against my face. I was filled with a sense of peace; all the fears and ignorance of the day seemed to drop away. This was the Hôtel des Oeillets, real, not the mirage we had held in front of us through the travelling; we had arrived.

"L'hôtel n'accepte pas les malades," said Madame Corbet.

"Does that mean she won't take sick people?" I asked Joss.

"I think it does."

The office at Les Oeillets was off the stairs, it was not big enough to be called a room; steps led up from the hall to an entresol with a landing and doors; the office was an annex to this landing, separated from it by a counter and brass grille. There was just room behind the, counter for a safe, a keyboard with pigeonholes for letters, and Madame Corbet's desk with its telephone and account books. Now we, Joss, Hester, Will-mouse, Vicky, and I, stood in front of the grille; Willmouse's eyes were just level with the counter; only the top of Vicky's hat showed.

The staircase was panelled in pale green, riddled with curi-ous holes, but the holes did not take away from its elegance.

The hall was elegant too. It was odd that we, who had never seen elegance before—though it was our favourite word— immediately recognized it—except Hester. "It isn't like the Metropole or Cavendish," she said regretfully. They were the big hotels on Southstone's grand parade, but instinctively I liked this better. The staircase made a graceful shape as it led up to the floor above. The banister rail was dark polished wood, the banisters thin and white: halfway up was a round window that showed a glimpse of trees, and in the wall were crystal wall lamps that matched the chandelier in the hall. We looked at that, amazed, for we had never seen a chandelier in a house. The hall had a squared marble floor; its chairs were gilt with faded brocade cushions; four small tables stood against the walls. "But they are only halves," said Willmouse in surprise. We had never seen console tables either.

In that hall our fibre suitcases looked cheap. We had other luggage even more vulgar: a basket, the bag that had held the oranges, a brown paper parcel of the Littles' Wellington boots, an untidy heap of raincoats with their belts hanging; and we all carried treasures. Joss's, of course, were neat, a drawing-board strapped to her wooden paintbox. Hester had her camera, Willmouse his scrapbooks and workbox packed up with Miss Dawn and Dolores, while Vicky had Nebuchadnezzar in a basket. Nebuchadnezzar was a pig made out of a potato, with matchstick eyes and legs; she had made him at school and carried him about ever since, though he was beginning to shrivel a little. "When he is quite shrivelled I shall eat him," said Vicky. Mother, sitting on a chair, had her hat on one side and the coat of her good suit wrongly buttoned; she leaned her head against the chair back and shut her eyes and her face seemed as mottled now as her leg. As for us, we were crumpled, untidy, and dirty; Hester's and Vicky's faces were streaked with dirt and tears; their socks had come down, and all our shoes were dusty. I could see that we were not at all the kind of family that would be an ornament to any hotel.

"I expect a doctor will come and take our mother to hospital," Joss said in English.

"L'hôtel n'accepte pas les enfants seuls."

"She won't take children by themselves."

"But if we are by ourselves?" said Hester.

Madame Corbet sat behind the grille with the hotel books spread out round her. On this hot evening she was wearing a black high-necked blouse; a black crochet shawl with bobbles was crossed on her shoulders. She wore a finger guard of stained celluloid and her face looked stained too with sallow marks; her hair was in two black snakes coiled in a knot on the top of her head and she had a moustache of heavy black down on which Willmouse, straining to look over the counter, had instantly fixed his eyes. All the time we were talking I saw him examining it.

Joss was desperate. I knew that by her white face and the bigness of her eyes. She had taken over Mother's capacious old handbag, which looked oddly big on her. "S'il vous plaît, aidez-nous," she said. I know how difficult it was for her to humble herself, but Madame Corbet only shrugged so that the topknot and the bobbles of her shawl danced. "Et qu'est-ce que je peux y faire, moi? Je ne suis pas la patronne. Je suis Madame Corbet, c'est tout." She said that as if to be Madame Corbet was something derogatory.

"If it is not your hotel, where is . . ." Joss consulted the paper Mr. Stillbotham had given us. "Where is Mademoiselle de Presle?"

"Mademoiselle Zizi? Elle va dîner au château de Méry."

Joss and I looked at each other. Did she say *going* out to dinner? In Southstone we had supper at seven o'clock; now it was nearly ten.

"Au château de Méry," repeated Madame Corbet impressively.

The maid who had helped with our luggage and who was now waiting on the stairs rolled up her eyes and crossed herself; she was pert and Madame Corbet spoke sharply.

"Y sont des amis . . ."

"'Amis' means friends," I told Hester. "Mademoiselle de Presle is going to a big house, a château, that might mean a castle, to friends."

"Des amis à Monsieur Eliot . . ." said the maid. Why did she say "Mr. Eliot's friends" so meaningly?

Madame Corbet ignored her. To us she said, "They say the President of the Board of Trade is to be there," and I thought, So! she can speak English.

"Then we can't see Mademoiselle de Presle?" asked Joss.

"Naturally not."

"But what can we do?"

Madame Corbet shrugged. "Vous feriez bien d'aller au commissariat. Oui, allez au commissariat."

Commissariat? What was that? We looked at one another, mystified. "Police," said the hotel boy Paul from his place on the landing. "Go police."

Joss's face flamed as though Madame Corbet had slapped it. "Come," she said to us.

We left the counter and followed Joss across the hall, walking round the two big Alsatian dogs who lifted their dark furred faces; one wagged its tail; it was the first sign of friendliness Les Oeillets had given us. Perhaps it was that that made Madame Corbet feel ashamed.

"Vous pouvez laisser les bagages," she said.

"No, thank you," said Joss.

This was proud but not very practical. The porter had gone and I do not know how we should have managed with Mother and the Littles, but at that moment the dogs stood up, wagging their tails more violently and looking towards a white door on the entresol landing. It opened and Mademoiselle Zizi and Eliot came out.

It was the first time we had seen anyone in tails. Uncle William had a dinner jacket, of course, but our vision had gone no further than that. I say "tails" because it was at Eliot we looked. It seems strange now that, seeing a man and a woman both in full evening dress, we looked at the man first, but there was no question about it. Hester gave a little gasp.

"Were you ever a sailor?" Joss asked Eliot afterwards. I knew what she meant; he was tall and brown and lean, as were sailors in magazine pictures. His eyes even had lines at the sides as if he had wrinkled them looking at the sun. "Were you a sailor?"

"Probably," said Eliot.

"Don't you know?" asked Hester, incredulous.

"I know I was a soldier," said Eliot. "Tinker, tailor, soldier, sailor, richman, poorman . . ." But Hester interrupted him.

"You can't have been everything," she said.

"I pretty well was," said Eliot.

We took it for granted that his eyes were blue. His hair was brown, a little grizzled. His face had curious high cheekbones, "from my Chinese grandmother," he told us solemnly. We believed him and it still seems to me now that his hands and feet were so small as to be Oriental. "I am descended from Genghis Khan," he was to tell us, and Hester asked, "Who was Genghis Khan?"

"A fearful Tartar," said Eliot, smoothing her hair.

His clothes were so impeccable—that was a word I liked and had taught to Willmouse—that they looked as if he had just bought them.

"Well, he had." Hester said that later. "Poor Eliot. He could never keep his clothes long."

"What do you mean?"

"He said so. He said, 'Pity, I like this coat. I hate to leave it.' That was his checked one; of course, he was thinking aloud. He did not know I was there. Toinette is always saying that his shirts and pyjamas are new."

That night he wore medals. "His?" Uncle William always said he doubted it but, "Of course they were his," we said indignantly.

He had a carnation in his buttonhole, a dark red one, and it seemed to symbolize Eliot for us. Why are flowers bought by men so much more notable than those bought by women? I do not know, but they are. Father brought flowers into the house but they were dried, pressed brown, the life gone out of them; with Eliot the flower was alive; we could smell its clove scent and it was heady.

Behind him came Mademoiselle Zizi. When we looked at her we were struck dumb with shyness because Mademoiselle Zizi was . . . "bare," whispered Hester. Arms, neck and shoulders, "and back and front," said Hester reluctantly. We did not know what little puritans we were until we saw Mademoiselle Zizi.

Privately I thought her very beautiful with her heavy dark red hair and eyes that seemed almost too enormous—like a sunflower's. They were blued—"on the *lids*," said Hester, surprised—and her mouth was very, very red. What there was of her dress was gauze, black.

I saw Willmouse looking at the dress critically at first, then satisfied. "That is a real dress," whispered Willmouse, "and what a smell!"

"Is the smell the lady?" asked Vicky. It had filled the hall as Mademoiselle Zizi came in.

They came down the steps from the landing, stopped at the sight of us, and it was then that Eliot said, "Good God! An orphanage!"

Joss was too angry to notice that he spoke in English.

"Don't worry," she said bitingly, "we are not staying." To us she said sharply, "Come on. We will take the luggage first and come back for Mother."

She walked past Eliot to the door, her painting things under her arm; she had picked up two suitcases; Vicky, carrying Nebuchadnezzar's basket, was holding to one of them. The rest of us followed, loyally staggering too. Paul went to open the door, but Eliot stepped forward.

"Where are you going this time of night?"

"To the police." Joss's nostrils were pinched with temper.

"The police? Why?"

"Because of you *French*," said Joss furiously.

"I'm not French, I'm English," said Eliot.

Mother must have heard that. She gave a moan and said, "Please." Eliot looked past us to her, and his face changed. "Zizi," he said, "she's ill."

He went quickly to Mother, bent down and took her hand, feeling it as he questioned her, but after that "Please" Mother did not speak again, and her head rolled against the chair.

"She's very ill, Zizi," he said. "We must help."

"But . . . our dinner." Her English was pretty and clipped.

"All the same."

"But we shall be late!"

"All the same." It sounded like a command. "Irène," he called to Madame Corbet, "ring Doctor Giroux," and to Mauricette, "Open the rooms."

I heard Madame Corbet pick up the telephone, the maid shrugged and went to the keyboard. Paul took the suitcases from Joss but Mademoiselle Zizi stayed where she had been, at the foot of the steps, her beautiful dress held up.

CHAPTER III

To wake for the first time in a new place can be like another birth. I think that to me it was perhaps more startling than to most people because, for as long as I could remember, I had waked each morning in the same bedroom in Belmont Road, that essentially English bedroom with its wallpaper faded to a grey-blue pattern; to the same white curtains and blue linoleum, the brown rug worn in places so that the white showed through the brown; to the same white enamelled iron beds, paisley eiderdowns, and the pictures that were framed prints from old supplements to the *Illustrated London News*. Uncle William and Mother had had those pictures when they were children but Joss had taken them down and put up a Chinese painting instead; she took that with her to Willmouse's room, and I brought the prints back. "Cecil is sentimental," said Joss.

There, in the early mornings, lying between sleeping and waking, I could hear and identify all the so ordinary early morning sounds: the milkman's pony, the paperboy's quick

steps, the thud as the paper dropped through the letter-box
into the hall, the postman—though there was not often anything for us—the cheeping of sparrows, the clock on the town
hall with its chimes, Mother's squirrel-quick little footsteps as
she went downstairs to pull the damper out so that the water
would be hot for our baths.

This morning my ears were filled with a high clear sound
broken into small sharp edges; it was a little while before I
knew it was from birds. The room was filled with dim light;
the ceiling was high and the walls far away, for it was a big
room. I made out the top of a green shutter and then saw that
the shutters ran from the ceiling to a floor of plain polished
boards without a rug. I was in an immense bed and beside me
lay Willmouse.

We had slept without pillows; mysteriously there had been
none on the beds and we were too shy to ask, besides "oreiller"
was a difficult word to pronounce; I remember how surprised
we were when we found the pillows in the wardrobe. I never
knew why Toinette kept them there.

The sheets felt dry and hot as if their cotton were brittle. I
swung my legs over the edge of the bed and slipped down; the
boards were cool under my feet as I walked to the window.
After a few moments I found how the shutters opened and
threw them back.

I was looking into the tops of the trees; at first I thought
the house was ringed with them, then I saw that it was only a
poplar in front of the window, filling the room with its sound,
and beyond it a single great tree that I thought was a willow,
though I had not known willows could grow as tall; through
its hanging branches I could see farther away serried rows

of fruit trees, some of them heavy with fruit. Perhaps it was this first sight that made me always think of the garden at Les Oeillets as green, green and gold as was that whole country-side of the Marne where, beyond the town, the champagne vineyards stretched for miles along the river, vineyards and cherry orchards, for this was cherry country too, famous for cherries in liqueur. Mother had been thinking of the battle-fields; she had not thought to inquire about the country itself; I am sure she had not meant to bring us to a luxury corner of France where the trees and the vines changed almost symboli-cally in the autumn to gold.

We were not to see that, nor did I know anything about it as I stood by the open window, yet, from the garden, I had a foretaste of that green and amber time and a sense of the countryside in the haze that lay around the town. I could not see the town behind the trees, only a glimpse of houses climb-ing a hill that had a building on it, a ruined castle or château with ramparts and a tower. The houses were yellow-white, jumbled below the ramparts. I guessed they spread down to what must be a river for there was the chugging sound of a boat. The chugging was near; the river, I thought, must be on the other side of the orchard.

Our rooms were on the second floor and if I looked directly down I could see a flight of iron steps with a scrolled iron railing leading from a terrace along the house into a garden that seemed to be made of gravel and small flower beds. I was to learn that Robert, the silent, cross gardener, spent all his time raking the gravel smooth, tidying the beds. There was a round bed in the middle which held an iron urn planted with geraniums, and smaller plots along the sides were bedded with flowers that even in that early light had violent colours. It looked a garden from one of our French grammar books, hideous and formal, but beyond it a low box-hedge bounded a wilderness of grass and shrubs and trees, bamboos, a monkey-puzzle smothered in creepers, and tangles of roses. Overgrown paths wound among them where white statues glimmered; some of the statues were broken, their arms and legs hacked off; one was lying on its side. Beyond the wilderness was what seemed to be an orchard, and in its high wall a blue door. As I looked at the door, a barge hooted from the river.

The garden was light but it was a young light without sun, clear and stained green by the shrubs and trees. The peace I had felt at the gates of Les Oeillets filled me again and I could have whistled like the birds for well-being and joy. Then, as I stood there in my pyjamas looking down, a man came down the iron steps. He was an old man with white hair and a small white beard; from above he looked nearly square. He wore blue cotton trousers, a white coat, and a beret—men wearing berets still looked strange to me. He was carrying many things: something that looked like an easel with long legs, a camp stool, a case, and a bulging white cotton umbrella, the kind of umbrella people put up outside their bathing chalets on the beach at Southstone. He seemed in a hurry; I watched him scurry across the gravel, disappear in the wilderness,' and caught a glimpse of him among the fruit trees. Then he was at the far blue door where he had to put everything down to open it.

"That was Monsieur Joubert," said Eliot when I asked him, "Monsieur Joubert going out to catch the first light."

"Who is Monsieur Joubert?"

"A painter."

A painter! Joss would like to hear that.

"A very famous painter," said Mademoiselle Zizi. "Even an ignorant little English girl should have heard of Marc Joubert."

"He didn't look famous," I said in defence. "He was wearing funny clothes and he looked . . ." I tried to think how to express his scurrying haste ". . . anxious."

"He probably was," said Eliot. "It's only for a short while that the light stays like that. I have a belief," and I remember Eliot sounded defiant, as if a belief were a strange thing to have, "that as soon as a human goes out into the morning it is spoilt—except a Monsieur Joubert or," and his eyes looked at us thoughtfully, "perhaps children."

"Do you like children so much?" asked Mademoiselle Zizi.

"I don't know any," said Eliot.

Now I watched Monsieur Joubert without knowing his name. The blue door shut with a distant bang and I heard another sound close beside me, in the next room, and I knew what had wakened me. It was Joss in the little room off our bedroom—she had chosen it though they had meant it for Willmouse—the sound was Joss having an attack.

"Nerves," Mother used to say of these, but Uncle William said they were bilious. Probably both were right. The attacks came at the most inconvenient times and, as I listened, the day began to foreclose on me; it must, I knew, be a difficult day, frightening, probably humiliating, and now Joss was useless. I went in, and she was as I knew I should find her, retching, her skin a curious green-yellow, her eyes looking as though they were bursting with pain. Now she would have to be in a darkened room for days, and I would have to be responsible for everything.

"Perhaps it was the soup," I said as I held her head.

"I—didn't—eat the soup." Though she was being sick as she said it I knew she was offended. That made me remember I was offended too. The maid Mauricette had brought up the soup in bowls on a tray after we had been bundled off to bed, Joss and I with Hester and Willmouse and Vicky—"and we are not Hester and Willmouse and Vicky," said Joss.

"I'm sorry. I made a mistake," Eliot said when I pointed this out to him—Joss refused to mention it. "You must remember we were all a bit confused." Eliot could be very charming; he smiled at Joss and put his hand on hers. "You won't forgive me?"

"No," said Joss and took her hand away.

Now, "Shall I get Mother?" I asked Joss.

"Don't be silly. There is a nun in her room."

"A *nun?*" Prickles of superstition swept over me. "Then . . . is she dying?"

"Don't be *si*-lly." But Joss's voice was fainter. "Lots of hospital nurses are nuns—especially in France."

"How do you know?"

"The Madame told me . . . I went in last night," but she had sunk from the washing-stand on to the bed and could not talk any more. In a moment she had to struggle up again. I helped her and when it was over she lay back, her skin clammy, her eyes closed. The washing-stand had only a heavy china basin and jug; there seemed to be no sloppail, only a strange object like an enamelled footbath or a doll's bath, on legs—we had not met a bidet before—and it was too shallow. "If you could get a basin or a bucket," Joss whispered, "I could manage in bed."

"From where?" I said, appalled.

"Downstairs. There must be one. Go and look."

"In someone else's house?"

"It isn't a house. It's a hotel."

"Supposing I meet someone . . ."

"You could ask them."

I shrank from it but I had to go. "What is the French for bucket?" I asked.

The stairs creaked as I came down though I crept carefully. I remember the surprise of the bullet holes; in the daylight I saw that the pale green paint was pocked with them. "Of course," Mademoiselle Zizi often explained. "They machine-gunned the stairs."

"And the marks are still there!" the visitors used to say in wonder.

"As you see." And Mademoiselle Zizi would smile with pride.

"If it were my house," Joss said, "I should have filled them up at once."

Now I came down cautiously because of the two dogs, but when I saw them I felt a coward. They were in the hall, chained each on a low bed; they knew I had been accepted the night before and they lifted their faces and moved their tails.

I had had another timid idea that Madame Corbet would be in the office but the grille was locked, the counter bare, and the hall was empty. Next to it on the right was a large open room with a bar and, at the garden end, what must have been a conservatory, leading through glassed doors to the terrace. The big room had small iron tables, and chairs painted green, coat-stands, tubs bound with brass and filled with sand for cigarette ends. The bar was covered with white dust sheets. On the left of the hall were doors and a sign that said "Restaurant." At the back was a baize-covered door that must, I thought, lead to the kitchen.

When I had pushed it open I did not have far to go. At the end of a short passage was a table stacked with flower vases and bowls. I took a bowl and, almost before the door had stopped swinging, was back into the hall, where I patted the dogs. I had turned upstairs when the white door on the landing opened and a man came out. He was wearing a silk patterned dressing-gown . . . like an actor's, I thought . . . leather slippers, and was smoking a cigarette. It was Eliot.

We both stopped abruptly. I knew how I must look, my raincoat bundled round me, blue and white striped pyjamas showing, bare feet, and my hair tied back with a blue ribbon like a baby's. Then I forgot about myself, staring at him. This was another Eliot than the kind Englishman of last night; someone cold and . . . ruthless, I thought. That was a strange word to come into my head when I did not know the meaning of "ruth." "Eliot's eyes are not blue," Hester was to say. "They are green-grey, like pebbles." Now, close to him on the stairs, I saw they were grey and coldly angry. "What are you doing down here?"

I showed the bowl. "Joss, my sister, is ill."

"God! Children!" he said. He put his hand behind him and closed the door, leaning against it. Then he was more kind. "Eaten too much?" he asked, but I, remembering Joss's offendedness, was stiff.

"She is not that kind of sister," I said and went on upstairs.

It was a day or two afterwards that, when for some reason we wanted Eliot, I said, "I shall fetch him," and crossed the hall to the landing and the white door.

"Where are you going?" asked Hester.

"To his room."

"That is not Eliot's room," said Hester. "That is Mademoiselle Zizi's."

CHAPTER IV

"Who let that man into my room?" asked Joss.

It was after tea on that first strange day—"only there wasn't any tea," said Vicky; we had not learned about the French children's goûter yet—it was what should have been after tea, that Eliot looked at us sitting forlornly round a table in the bar and asked, "Shouldn't there be one more of you?" Then he had asked me to take him upstairs to see Joss.

She lay stiff and flat in the bed while he was in the room; her hair was spread on the pillow and in the gloom of the closed shutters her sick face looked small as a turnip-goblin's. She might have been any age and he was as familiar as he would have been with someone as young as Vicky.

"Are you a better girl?"

She answered him in monosyllables. "Yes."

"Cheer up. You will be well soon."

"Yes."

"Is there anything you want? You can have it, you know."

"No."

I think Eliot did not know quite what to do. "You are not worrying too much about your mother? We are taking care of her." No answer. Presently he went out and Joss reared up on her pillow.

"Who let him in?"

"I . . . did."

"How dared you?"

"But . . . he is in charge of us."

"Cha—" She looked at me in astonishment. "Who said so?"

"Mother. She asked him."

"She always was an *idiot*!" said Joss.

The sickness had started again. I waited while she retched miserably into the bowl by the bed. At last she lay back exhausted and, wearily accustomed, I brought her face flannel and wiped the sweat off her face and hands, and dried them. I knew her skin hurt by the way she winced but, as soon as she could speak, she croaked, "You must . . . tell Mother."

I stood by the bed, holding the towel, and cleared my throat. It seemed to have a frog in it too. "I can't tell Mother," I said. "Joss, they—they have taken her to the hospital."

Joss had been too ill to know but it had been a split day, split between Les Oeillets and Belmont Road.

As soon as I was dressed I had gone and knocked softly on Mother's door. It had opened and Joss had been right, the nun was there. She was dressed in white with a black veil, girdle, and crucifix. I had not been close to a nun before and gazed at her startled. She put her finger to her lip and shook her head. Pinpricked all over with fear, I tiptoed away.

Then Hester and Vicky came in asking for breakfast. "There isn't any," I said quailing, but they insisted there was plenty downstairs and in the end I had to take them and find the dining room. Willmouse had gone there already. In the big room I tried to be as travelled and self-contained as even Joss could have wished but there was Hester's clear unabashed voice and Vicky's obstinacy about food; she was as stubbornly British as John Bull. "I want breakfast," she said. I gave her coffee and a croissant. "This isn't breakfast," said Vicky. "I want an egg."

"You can't have eggs for breakfast in France."

"Of course you can," Eliot was to say. "Lots of people ask for them." He added that I was not to be a travel snob, but I was a travel snob and an age snob too. Vicky was, of course, too much for me; as usual, she got her own way and I had to ask not only for an egg but for babyish milk and jam.

It was Paul who brought them—I soon learned that Mauricette would seldom bother herself to wait on us. Paul deliberately put the milk and jam at my place. "Essuie-toi l'bec avec ta bavette," he said. I did not guess he had said, "Wipe your mouth on your bib," until I got upstairs and looked up "bavette" in our pocket Larousse, but I knew it was something derogatory and I looked sternly at this Paul.

He was a tall, thin, dirty, and greasy boy dressed in blue cotton trousers and a ragged shirt. He wore the white apron and the grey-white canvas shoes—we had not learned yet to call them espadrilles—he had worn last night. His shirt had the sleeves rolled up; his elbows looked as sharp as knives, and when he turned his back the shoulder blades stuck out. He had lank, yellow hair with a lock falling over his forehead and his face had hollows in the cheeks. I did not know about Paul in those days but even then, in my carelessness and ignorance,

I was worried by his face. We had come to see the battlefields
and, though we did not know it, this face was a part of them.

Who was Paul? Nobody knew. Even his name might have
belonged to almost any nationality; it was one of the few that
hardly change in pronunciation from one country to another.
Paul could have been English, German, French, Austrian,
Russian. His mother, Madame Corbet said contemptuously,
had "gone with the soldiers."

"Gone where?" asked Hester but nobody answered that.

"Our father's a botanist," Hester told Paul. "What's yours?"

"Un troufion," said Paul, and when we looked mystified he
pretended to march and salute.

"Oh, a soldier!" I said.

"What was his name?" asked Hester, but the father did not
seem to have had a name. One day Paul said, "J'avais une p'tite
soeur."

"A little sister?" By then Hester was beginning to understand.

"Une mulâtre," said Paul carelessly and, seeing we did not
understand that either, he said, "Une négresse," and showed
half on his finger.

"Negro? But you are not mulat—what you called it," we
said, puzzled, and asked, "Where is she, your sister?"

Paul shrugged.

"Don't you know?"

He shook his head. "Elle a disparu."

Hester looked inquiringly at me. "She disappeared," I said.

"Does he mean dead?" asked Hester.

I tried him with that. "Morte?" I asked sympathetically.

"Perdue," said Paul. "Pssts," and he made as if he threw
something away.

"But you don't lose *sisters*." Paul's silence said clearly that you did. We felt dizzy.

He had been found in the American camp when it was broken up; the soldiers themselves had found him and been kind. When they went home to America he was taken to the alms-house, the Hôtel-Dieu. "God's hotel?" asked Hester. "That should have been good," but Madame Corbet said it was where they put old people waiting to die, and lunatics and badly treated children from the courts. "That doesn't *sound* good," said Hester doubtfully.

Madame Corbet did not seem disturbed. "Where are they to go in a little town like this?" she asked. She added that Paul was bad and ran away, the police brought him back, and, "Mademoiselle Zizi, out of her kindness, let him work here."

It did not seem very kind. As we were to find out, Paul worked from six in the morning—or before, if there was a party for breakfast—until midnight—or after if there were dinners. He had plenty to eat—everyone near Monsieur Armand, the chef, had that—but Paul's sleeping place was in a cupboard under the stairs, and had not even a window; the bed was planks with a straw mattress, there was a dirty pillow and the kind of blanket given to dogs.

"But all that was no reason to make a set at me," I said afterwards, but it seemed it was. I think now our coming, so unaware, so pink and protected, gave Paul a smart he had not known before, and particularly when Joss was near him, every spot of grease, each broken black nail stood out, and the smell of him, in which he lived unnoticing, stank.

The first morning we knew none of this and I looked at him, my chin high, then coldly turned my eyes away. It was not done as Joss would have done it, but it was the best I could do. I spread Vicky's croissant with jam and poured out her cup of milk; then, copying a big Frenchman in the corner, I dipped my own croissant in the dark bitter coffee and ate it like that. It tasted nasty but at least it was French.

After breakfast I sent Hester, Willmouse, and Vicky out to explore. I watched them as they scampered down the alleys of the orchard and my legs itched to run too; still, in spite of my teens, that urge to run and scamper and roll like a colt would rise in me, but Paul was watching; besides, with Mother and Joss ill I felt as weighted with cares as Uncle William. I went out on to the terrace and stood at the top of the iron steps, holding the rail that was already warm from the sun.

I could not feel an Uncle William for long. All around me rose the sounds of this, my first real French morning. Overhead the voices of two women talked. From Joss's window that, unlike ours, faced the road, I had seen them earlier come in through the gate. They were the daily maids and now they flung mattresses over the sills upstairs, shook dusters and brooms. One called from her window to the other, "Toinette, la clé du quatorze," and the other shrilled back, "En bas, Nicole, sur le tableau." Why should that have ravished me? I do not know, but it did. Water was running in what I guessed was the kitchen because of the clatter of china and a man's big voice shouting orders. Mauricette was singing in the dining room, a nasal little song,

"Je l'ai tellement dans la peau,
C'est mon homme.
Que j'en suis marteau,
C'est ... mon ... homme."

A typewriter clacked in the office. I looked over the garden to the green dew of the wilderness and orchard, the sun haze beyond, and I could stay in no longer; slowly I went down the steps, across the gravel, past the flower beds and through a gap in the box hedge. Stepping in dew, my head in the sun, I walked into the orchard and, before I knew what I had done, reached up to touch a greengage. It came off, warm and smooth into my hand. I looked quickly round but no one came, no voice scolded and, after a moment, I bit into the ripe golden flesh. Then I ate another, and another, until, replete with fruit and ecstasy, I went back to my post.

There was no sign of Mademoiselle Zizi but presently Eliot came out. He was aloof and unapproachable. How did I know then that he had these times? I do not know but, as if the first greengage had been an Eden apple, I was suddenly older and wiser and did not try to speak to him. He passed me as if I did not exist and went out into the sun. He was wearing linen trousers, a dark blue open-necked shirt. Mauricette ran out with a deck chair for him but he was curt with her. How wonderful to be as curt in French as in English! The ecstasy faded. I was suddenly depressed again. How inferior we were; our family had never been anywhere at all and did not know anything.

Then Paul came out and jerked his thumb over his shoulder for me to go to the office. Madame Corbet sent me to fetch our passports and Hester bobbed up and told about Uncle William.

Monsieur William John Bullock, wrote Mademoiselle Zizi on a slip of paper; then she opened the grille and the flap of the counter and came out. She ran upstairs and her heels sounded very determined as she crossed the landing to Mother's room. My heart sank and I pushed Hester away in disgust and went up too.

Mother was a prisoner in the bed; a cage had been put over the bad leg and she lay on her back, her eyes looking this way and that, past Mademoiselle Zizi, past the nun; then she saw me in the doorway and beckoned me. I slipped past the foot of the bed and knelt down. Mother clutched me and whispered but the whisper was so thick and blurred that I could hardly understand it. "Get the Englishman," whispered mother. "That man who was English."

Mademoiselle Zizi's ears were sharp. "No! You are not to," she cried, but I had slipped out.

When Eliot came I knew how good he was. "Not good," said Hester, who was exact. "A good person would not have done it. Not good, kind," which was nearer our hearts.

He came in, looking tall in that room of women.

"Mais Eliot, je t'en prie . . ."

"Wait, Zizi." He bent down and Mother caught his hand. I knew how hot hers were from when she had held me and her eyes were full of pain. "Is there anything I can do for you?" asked Eliot.

"Don't let them." It was the same thick whisper. "Don't let them."

"Eliot, this is nothing to do with you."

"Please, Zizi." He bent down lower. "Don't let them what?"

Mother could look very like Hester. "Don't let them send for William."

I saw his lips twitch. "But . . ."

"He will say 'I told you so,'" whispered Mother.

"I see," said Eliot. "Yes, I understand."

"But she has to go to hospital," cried Mademoiselle Zizi. "Bon Dieu! Et si elle allait mourir?" She went on so fast that I could not keep up, but Eliot, while the stream of French went on, kept Mother's hand.

"Why did he consent? A fellow like that?" Uncle William said afterwards. "It wasn't in keeping."

"Perhaps," said Joss privately to me, "Eliot once had an Uncle William."

"But what can I tell Irène?" said Mademoiselle Zizi.

I think she and Eliot spoke in English sometimes because they did not want the servants to understand, but they mixed it, sometimes one would ask a question in English, the other answer it in French, or the other way round. "What can I tell Irène?"

"That you can put two into a single room and charge for both."

"Eliot, you are laughing at me."

"Not laughing, predicting."

"But, can they pay?" asked Mademoiselle Zizi. "They do not look as if they had much."

"If they can't I will."

"Have you so much money, Eliot?"

He did not tell her. "It comes and goes," he said and there was the sound of a kiss; but Eliot said something else, something odd and . . . not pleasant, I thought. "Those children can be useful."

"How useful?"

"Stop people talking."

"Let them talk," said Mademoiselle Zizi.

"Don't be silly, Zizi. This is a little town and you have to live in it. The children will give me a reason for being here. After all, now I'm their guardian. They can be camouflage."

I did not like us being camouflage and he was right about the rooms. Hester and Vicky slept on each end of a single bed, and Joss was in our dressing-room, which was not really a bedroom at all. We were not allowed to use the bathrooms and our only lavatory was the one we called the Hole, because it was in a cubbyhole opening off the stairs; there was no pedestal or seat, only a pan in the floor and two places to put one's feet, "à la turque" Paul called it but it was awkward for someone as small as Vicky and ignominious for big girls. "And it smells the stairs," said Hester. Madame Corbet charged us for towels and soap; when I went that first morning to the desk to ask for some lemon water for Joss, Madame Corbet already had two pages on the ledger marked 15, 16, and 16A and there were several entries in her spider-fine writing. The lemon would be written in at once.

Paul kept the bar in the afternoons and Madame Corbet called to him to get it. "Alors vous restez?" he asked, looking me over.

"Yes, we are staying," I said coldly. I added sarcastically in French—I was determined to speak French to Paul—that I hoped it would not derange him.

He shrugged and Paul's shrug was indescribably rude. "Les enfants trouvés, y faut b'en s'en occuper, hein?" he said, and turned to take the slip for the lemon to the desk before he gave the glass to me.

I had caught "found children," that means "strays," I thought—strays! and as he went he pulled my hair.

There was no one in the hall but ourselves, no one to remind me I was big, almost grown up. Suddenly I had had enough of Paul. I ran after him and hit him as hard as I could on the jaw.

He was so surprised that he almost fell; the lemon water went spinning across the hall, his long legs slithered, and his apron slipped as he clutched at the newel-post on the steps leading to the landing; then, holding to the post, he bent forward and looked at me; the lock of hair had fallen farther over his eyes and they gleamed through it like an animal's. "So," said Paul. "So."

"Yes. So," I said.

He came at me but I was waiting. Paul was tall but he was gangling, while I was a Bullock and all Bullocks were solid and strong. I got one more hit in on his chest, then his arms wore like a flail hitting me and he knocked me over; in a moment we were both on the ground, rolling and scratching. I remember him pounding my head on the marble, when Madame Corbet screamed and people came running. I saw Mauricette's legs, black skirt, and frilled apron, before my own blood blinded me as I dug my thumbs into Paul's throat until we were taken like kittens by the scruffs of our necks and shaken apart.

It was the chef. I could smell the grease on his white clothes and had a startling view of his fat cheeks, polished black moustache, and high white cap seen through the tears that were stupidly pouring from my eyes.

Eliot's voice came. "Let them go," he said, and the chef dropped us—again like kittens—and we stood in the middle of them all, breathing hard and glaring at each other. Mauricette held a table napkin to my nose; it was not her table napkin and Madame Corbet snatched it away. Eliot looked at us, amused, and passed me his handkerchief; I was very much ashamed.

I thought he would say something about my being a girl, even a young lady, but he did not. I suppose that to him we were two young animals. "Next time," he said, "fight in the garden. This is a lady's house," and he said it in French for Paul, "Vous êtes ici chez une dame comme il faut." Paul made a rude noise. "Chez une dame comme il faut," repeated Eliot; his voice was so peremptory that Paul stood up straight, "et vous vous tiendrez comme il faut."

Late that evening I met Paul again. At dusk the garden greenness took on a richer light, as if the rays of the sunset stayed there prisoned by the walls; the leaves glimmered and the grass; the broken statues that were chill and white in the morning turned almost to gold. Robert had ceased his raking and gone home. The dogs lay out on the warm gravel, voices came more gently from the house, everything was filled with peace. I was still in the habits of Belmont Road and, sore as I was, with my swelled nose, I had come to find. Vicky— I guessed she was with Monsieur Armand whom she had instantly adopted—to put her to bed.

Paul was sitting on a stone step outside the kitchen. I did not know whether to pass him or go back through the house; that would have looked a retreat and I decided to pass him, though I was trembling. As I came nearer he stood up.

All right. If you want to fight, I thought, but.. . . "Please, mees," he said and pulled out a crumpled paper packet of the horrible-smelling cigarettes he smoked, and held them out to me.

I expect I blushed—no one had ever offered me a cigarette before—then I saw it was not condescension; he was offering them as to an equal. I took one. I did not know at all how I should smoke it, but was immensely flattered. Paul struck a match for me; I took my first puff and choked; he patted me on the back, and then we were sitting down together on the steps.

Vicky was hours late going to bed. "Well, she is in France; she must do as French children do," I said. Belmont Road was disappearing fast.

When I went up to Joss, she drew away across the bed and said, "Whew!"

"It's a Gauloise, a French cigarette." I tried to sound careless but Joss's look remained cold and she said icily, "You seem to have settled in here very quickly."

CHAPTER V

We had settled. After that first disrupted day we might have been in Vieux-Moutiers all our lives. Why did we like it so much? "Because it was not Southstone," said Uncle William testily. There was truth in that; after Southstoné this old French town, drenched that year in sun, seemed especially beautiful. Southstone had not grown; it had been built in a few years as a watering place. Its red brick houses with slated roofs stood in well-ordered asphalt roads, planted neatly with laburnum and bright pink may trees, each cased in a stand of wire netting; it had a Winter Garden for concerts, a skating rink, covered tennis courts, swimming baths, tea rooms, and large shops. Its cliffs were cut up into municipal gardens, its foreshore into a parade with a bandstand and pier, a Round Tower, clock golf course, and an aquarium. Vieux-Moutiers beside its wide peaceful river was centuries old; its upper and lower town had grown slowly, haphazardly, or crumbled away with disuse. It was so small that one could not get lost, though it had a maze of tiny cobbled lanes around the Place where the market was held twice a week in front of the Hôtel de Ville, as we learned to call the town hall.

The Hôtel de Ville was sixteenth-century and the upper town was crowned by the monastery whose ramparts I had seen from my window; besides a monastery it was a prison and held the old Donjon St. Pierre. There was a gate through which Saint Joan had ridden with Charles VII and I heard an American visitor read out from his guide book: "She had probably heard Mass in the chapel, and the horse block from which she mounted her horse still stands in the courtyard."

"Saint Joan? Then was she a person?" I asked. "I thought she was a saint."

"A saint is a person, you little silly," said Eliot, "that is the whole point."

Nobody told us about Vieux-Moutiers. Its history dawned on us as we overheard the visitors talking, or wandered by ourselves in the streets. The hospital, for instance. There was a notice over the stairs that we saw when we went to leave the bunches of wild flowers we picked for Mother. "Essuyez vos pieds, S.V.P." said the notice, and we carefully wiped our feet while we spelled out the rest: "Erigée en 1304 par la grâce de Jeanne de Navarre, épouse de Philippe le Bel." Our mother, *our* mother, was in a hospital built by a queen. I wished I were married to Philip the Beautiful.

In the upper town there was a cream-washed house with marigold-coloured, patched stains on its walls; by its front door was a plaque. A poet had lived there, a famous one, and when we read his name the classrooms at St. Helena's came back, my punishments, Hester reciting at the school concert. "*That* poet lived *here*." I did not think a poet had ever lived in

Southstone; it would be almost better to be married to a poet than to Philippe le Bel, and I took a flake from the cream-crusted walls to keep forever.

It was altogether a poet's town. Monsieur Joubert made us see that; he was working on two canvases, a morning one and one that he began after four o'clock when the light turned more gold. Looking at those paintings, watching as they slowly came to life, we saw the colours of the houses along the river bank and up the hill, the faint varyings of the shabby plaster, the pink and grey-green of the paint as it blistered on doors and shutters; I do not think there was a newly painted house in the whole town. We saw the shadows of the river, the black, white, and scarlet reflections of a barge eddying in the water, reflections of houses, trees, fishermen, children. Up above were the ruins of the monastery walls, their old stone turned a honey-yellow; the air was hazed with the town smoke against the sky. There were other colours: grains of grey and white that were pigeons and cats, the unexpected pink of an apron, a man's blue overalls, a jug, a cask, a child's toy; and there were sounds: the sound of the bells, of hammering from the boatyards, the hoot of a barge, the land hooter of the Brass Instruments Factory behind the town and, nearer, the cries of children bathing in the Plage des Saules.

In Vieux-Moutiers we were foreigners, which was more comfortable than being odd; the town was accustomed to tourists and nobody stared at us; we had achieved an obscurity that was strangely restful.

In Southstone our family circle had been five children alone with Mother. Our importance had receded only on Father's rare visits; Uncle William and his friends were as

uninteresting as the dead to us and children's doings, prob-
lems, ideas, and jokes had filled all our horizons. At Les
Oeillets we were as insignificant as grass under trees, under
the light and shadow of the grown-ups.

We had, too, been chiefly with girls and women, and
had been ruled by Mother who made a private child's world
for us; now suddenly we were surrounded by a public and
almost rude life. Madame Corbet told us not to go beyond
the gates at night because on the bridge into the town and
along the canal behind the Plage, sometimes there were
drunken men; we often heard their uncertain singing. Monsieur Joubert was painting a picture—a picture to hang in
a public gallery—of Robert's wife, suckling her baby. In the
kitchen we saw Paul pull Mauricette down on his lap and run
his hand up under her skirt; then Monsieur Armand would
turn round and give Paul a box on the ear and pull Mauricette to him and kiss her himself. "With those moustaches it
must prick," said Hester, which was a little girl's view, while
I had become as stretched and as sensitive as an Indian with
his ear to the ground, or as an insect's feeler or the needle in
a compass, to these doings. The sound of those loud kisses
seemed to go on and on in my ears; but that was nothing to
the way I watched how Mademoiselle Zizi would catch at
Eliot as he went by, and how he would kiss her hand or her
arm or her neck, sometimes her mouth. Eliot and Mademoiselle Zizi—and Madame Corbet—made an intense drama
for me.

It was Paul who told us about the drama. We could
speak little French, he had no more than a word or two
of American English, and yet Paul, as he sat with us on

the kitchen steps those summer evenings, was like a flood-lamp, illuminating everyone at Les Oeillets in the most gar-ish possible colours.

When I say "us" I mean Hester and me. Hester seemed to have moved up to become to me what I had been to Joss, a second self, a substantial shadow. Willmouse and Vicky had other interests. France and Mademoiselle Zizi had given Will-mouse new ideas and he was busily making a new collection; his atelier was a grass bank in the orchard under a cherry tree. Vicky had attached herself to Monsieur Armand, who gave her tidbits from morning to night. If Joss had not still been ill we should not have seen as much of Paul—"I do not talk to kitchen boys," she said, which explained why she was so ignorant—but her bout of sickness would not stop. "It is the shock," said the doctor. It was more than shock; she had one of her womanly times; "Eve's curse" we called it. It was as if she was being changed, sloughing off the old Joss like a skin. The doctor, whom we had learned to call Monsieur le Directeur from our visits to the hospital, came to see her twice and talked of moving her to be with Mother; in French hospitals, it seemed, there was a bed for a relation in private rooms. "But your mother is too ill," said Madame Corbet. She added that we were all a great nuisance.

There was little we could do for Joss. I made her bed and brought her barley drinks; Toinette took her cups of thin soup called "bouillon"; Eliot looked in on her every night for a moment; for the rest she lay in the darkened room and told us to leave her alone. It was an odd world without Joss or Mother; every day Hester and I wrote notes to Mother, and the Littles collected bunches of flowers which we all carried over the bridge to the hospital, passing a café called the Giraffe where Eliot often went for a drink. I do not know if Mother read our notes but not much of ourselves went into them; it was not that we did not care—at moments every day we cared abominably and were often frightened and lost—but Mother seemed to have become remote from us. That was just as well; sometimes I was a little uneasy and thought, If Mother knew what we talk about . . . but she did not know and I crushed the uneasiness down.

Hester asked Paul most of the questions. "Why does Madame Corbet hate us?"

She did hate us. She even wrote the figures into our account as if the pen could poison the paper; we watched in dread for her topknot to bob up over the grille and a reproof to be rapped out. Not even Vicky escaped. "Pourquoi est-ce qu'elle nous déteste?"

"Parce-que c'est Eliot qui a tout arrangé."

"Eliot?"

"Si."

"Then does she hate Eliot?"

"Si."

Paul's "Si" seemed to steal into my bones and stay there; it was sinister but exciting.

"*Hates* Eliot? Elle déteste Eliot?" I said while Hester's calm, little-girl voice went on, "Why does she hate Eliot?"

The answer came back, "Parce qu'elle en tient pour Mademoiselle Zizi," and, seeing I did not understand, "She lov Mademoiselle Zizi."

"A lady love a *lady*?"

We did not believe it, but, "Si," said Paul.

Now we had been told we saw it for ourselves. The topknot did not only come up to watch us; it spied on every movement of Mademoiselle Zizi.

Every evening we sat there on the steps—Paul with his Gauloise, his thin knees pointed under his apron—and from the garden, where twilight was falling, came that flower-sweet scent. I had always meant to go and look for its bush, find the flower, and instinctively I knew it was a better idea than to sit listening to this. The kitchen dustbins stood by the steps, the smell of their refuse filled our nostrils. That seemed symbolic and often I half rose, then sat down again on the warm stone. If Paul had the end of a bottle of wine, he would pass it to Hester, who would tip it up, take a mouthful, and pass it on to me; I would take one and hand it to Paul. "How disgusting!" said Joss when I told her.

"It isn't. We wipe the top on Paul's apron."

"Ouch!" said Joss and looked as if she would be sick again.

Once, after I had taken such a drink, with the dark vinegar taste of the wine in my mouth, I had said, "I think Mademoiselle Zizi is in love with Eliot."

There were empty bottles by the dustbin; one of them had gold foil on its neck. Paul stripped the foil off, shaped it into a round, and handed it to me. "Tu ne l'as pas volée," he had said gravely as he gave it to me for a medal.

Evening after evening Hester took up the saga. "Does Eliot love—aime—Mademoiselle Zizi?"

"Pas lui," said Paul and laughed. "Not him."

If the "Si" had stolen into my bones, the laughing woke them up. "They should never have let you talk to that boy!" Everyone said that afterwards; it was not Paul who was at

fault but my own thoughts. Coming from our Eden world
of Belmont Road I was like a young novice horse who jumps
too high, while Paul had been born an imp of the world,
the real world. To him all this was entirely natural; that was
what women were for. "J'avais quatorze ans quand j'ai fait
l'amour la première fois," he told me. At fourteen! I looked at
him suspiciously, but he was not boasting. He was far more
interested in lorries. "Renault, Berliet, Willème," he said as if
they were unimaginably beautiful names, and looked away
across the garden, his face soft with his dream. He could
not know that when he told me, small prickles seemed to be
breaking out all over me and the backs of my knees felt hot.
I had to persist. "You mean . . . you made love? When you
were *fourteen*?"

He laughed and put his arm round my neck, his hand
under my dress. I jumped as, quite casually and calmly, he
felt my breasts, but he took his hand away. "Deux petits citrons," he said and laughed. Citrons! Lemons! He laughed
again at the outraged look on my face and, with his finger,
tapped my nose as one would a little animal if it were too
eager. There was no doubt about it. It was I, not Paul, who
was bad.

I could not help it; it was a stain spreading through my
bones. I began to wonder about bones; Vicky's, I thought,
must be like a chicken's, pearly-pink and blue with a little clear
red. Monsieur Joubert's, for some reason, seemed to me the
same as Vicky's—perhaps they would not take a stain. "Well,
he is busy," said Joss when I expounded this to her. Paul's and
Hester's seemed red too, clean and honest; Joss's I did not
know about and would not have dared to inquire. I wondered

CHAPTER VI

"Eliot est un vrai mystère," said Paul. Yes, a great mystery, I thought, and sighed.

One of the oddest things about Eliot was that he had nothing that helped us to understand what kind of person he was. Everyone else had things, "toi, et moi, moi qui parle," said Paul. That was true. Mademoiselle Zizi had her bottles and jars, her scents and dresses; Madame Corbet had her crucifix and beads, I had seen them on her chest of drawers; Paul had his pictures of lorries, Berliet and Willème, pasted up in his cupboard, just as we had our treasures. "Mais Monsieur Eliot, il n'a rien," Paul said, not even a photograph or a paper, and even in Eliot's drawers, Paul told us, were only clothes folded up.

"You mean you look in other people's drawers?" we said, shocked.

"Si," said Paul cheerfully. Eliot had nothing, nothing to tell about himself.

"He has books," I objected. "I cut them for him." I liked doing it, it was a labour of love to cut the interminable pages of those paper-bound French novels. "But when he has finished them he throws them away," I had to admit.

"I cut them too," said Hester and she added, "but he has something, his beautiful paper knife."

I had never seen a paper knife like Eliot's. We thought it was silver but I suppose now it was steel, thin, about twelve inches long. "Thirteen," said Eliot, "my lucky number." Its blade was sharp-pointed with bevelled edges. "Be careful," said Eliot when we cut the pages, "don't let the Littles have it, it's sharp." It was. I remember once I dropped it point down on the grass; it went in and stayed upright.

It had a ring at the top with strange lettering. "Chinese," said Eliot.

"Where did you get it?" asked Hester, and Eliot said dramatically, "From my ancestor, Genghis Khan."

When we were with Eliot all that Paul told us disappeared—or was confirmed, confirmed as a part of life; we no more thought and wondered about it than we should have wondered about Eliot brushing his teeth.

He had us in excellent order, even Vicky. Though we were often a chorus, following him, we kept our distance when told. The hotel had its own bathing place, a cove in an inlet of the river made by a small island a few hundred yards along the bank; it was screened by bulrushes and hazels and shaded by big willow trees; when Eliot had lunched in the hotel he would sun-bathe in the cove afterwards, lying on its sand; "imported sand," he told us. "The Marne has, only gravel." He would not strip but let the sun soak through his clothes, his head and eyes shielded by an old yachting cap.

Then we stayed respectfully at a distance, which is what he meant us to do. He would seldom pick himself up until we had gone in for the goûter we owed to Paul. Paul gave us our food and at four o'clock had taken to coming to the kitchen door and whistling; I think we should have heard that whistle for miles. The goûter was delicious, though I do not know how we held it as well as all the other food; we were beginning to eat as much as the French themselves. Paul would take one of the long thin loaves called "baguettes," chop eight or ten inches off it, split that, spread the split with butter and clap in ham or jam or a slab of chocolate from the show case in the hall.

"But won't Madame Corbet. . . ?"

Paul made a rude noise and pretended to write with his hand; it was true, Madame Corbet behind the grille was entering the chocolate in the ledger.

Even for Eliot we would not have missed our goûter, but it was a long-drawn-out time, for Monsieur Armand had taken to making us pay for it. "Il faut payer," he would say gravely. "Little dogs must sing for their supper." He used to make Vicky, who sometimes lisped, say an old tongue-twister: "Combien sont ces six saucissons? Ces six saucissons sont six sous. Six sous, ces six saucissons? Mais ces six saucissons sont trop chers."

Four o'clock was Monsieur Armand's rest time; the lunches were finished, the kitchen was tidy, and it was not time yet to begin dinners. Then he sat at the table by the window, where the light was made green by the vine, and he read the newspaper, and drank a bottle of wine. He was very comfortable, his shoes off, his cap on the dresser; Vicky sat on the table by him and the kitchen cat, Minette, curled herself in the patch of

sun at his feet. It always amused Monsieur Armand to hear us
talk—he thought English an excruciatingly funny language—
and he had taken to making me, every day, translate some passage in the newspaper. I learned more French in the kitchen
at Les Oeillets than even in the punishments at St. Helena's.

That kitchen was a pleasant place; its whitewashed walls
were made green near the window by the vine, and orange-
gold near the fire; the light caught reflections in the rows of
copper pans that hung down the middle of the room. Below
them were the working tables with hot shelves above them
from which Mauricette took the dishes on the dining-room
side as Monsieur Armand and Paul put them in from the
other.

Behind the tables was the great stove of iron with polished steel handles and hinges. There were two sinks, a big
one and a smaller for washing up silver and glass and petits
déjeuners. In the next room was the machine for ice cream,
the marble slabs for making pâtisserie, and the small store of
vegetables; beyond that was the big store, where meat, poultry,
fish, and oysters were kept; Monsieur Armand took out what
was needed once each day. The live fish were in tanks outside.
There was a spit over an open fire at the end of the room, a red
bricked floor, and always a good smell of cooking onions, new
bread, coffee, and wine. In the afternoons Toinette and Nicole
would be talking gently in the scullery as they peeled potatoes
or cut beans or else there would be a smell of singeing and
hot linen as they ironed in the linen room along the passage.
Mauricette would wander in and out from the garden, her
apron off, and take a sip from Monsieur Armand's glass, while
Paul would pause in his work to tease her, or they would both

listen gravely to my reading. I do not know what newspaper Monsieur Armand read, but the bits he gave me were always sensational. "Que veut dire 'belle-mère'?" I would ask.

"Wife mother," said Monsieur Armand making a face.

"Oh, mother-in-law!" And I would read, "Mother-in-law hits husband with hatchet," or, "Baby girl found dead in trunk in—'grenier,' qu'est-ce que c'est?" but they could not make me understand and I had to look it up; the baby girl had been found in the attic.

Monsieur Armand seemed to think these horrors were good for me, which was odd because he was very particular what Paul said when we were near—he did not know what we talked of on the steps—and if Paul used swear words Monsieur Armand would smack his head. When Vicky's rosy little mouth said, "Merde!" and, "Ordure," he washed it out with a piece of kitchen soap, but when I read, "Thieves entice young wife while accomplice takes twenty thousand francs' worth of rings and brooches," or, "Soldiers tie schoolgirl on bed," he would chuckle with delight.

Sometimes we chafed because we knew when we raced back to the cove Eliot would be gone. He liked to walk along the bank undisturbed—perhaps to get away for a little while from his female admirers; sometimes he would walk downstream into the town and cross the bridge to the Giraffe. We would go back to the house and wait faithfully to see if he wanted us when he came in.

"I like that man," said Vicky, which was surprising because Eliot never gave her anything to eat and she was allowed to trot round after Monsieur Armand who gave her plenty; in her time at Les Oeillets Vicky grew very fat. She did not trot round after Eliot—none of us would have dared to do that—but when he noticed us, as he did quite often in an absent-minded way, she would give up the kitchen, the slivers of chicken and spoonfuls of cream, and stay where he was likely to be.

"And I like him," said Willmouse. "He is the only person I know except Mother who has never laughed at me."

That was the first time I knew Willmouse minded being laughed at. Then he was brave, this odd little brother of mine; it was strange how having a stranger added to the family made one look at its members with different eyes.

Eliot treated Willmouse with particular seriousness. He would look at Miss Dawn's and Dolores' new dresses, examining them and criticizing carefully. He bought Willmouse a book from Paris, not a fashion magazine but a big book of old masters. "Study them," he told Willmouse, "especially the primitives; they will give you a sense of drapery and colour." Willmouse only nodded but his eyes kindled.

"But books like that cost a fortune!" cried Madame Corbet.

"Not a fortune, just a bit," said Eliot.

"But for a child!"

"This child needs it."

Hester did not say what she felt but she had used up the last film in her Brownie on Eliot. Too shy to ask, she had crept up on tiptoe and taken a snapshot of him as he slept in his deck chair and spent the last of her travelling francs on having it developed at La Maison Kodak. She had shown the photograph to no one but stuck it on cardboard, with a cardboard stand, and made a frame of the dried white shells we found along the river; it stood on her chest of drawers, though she hid it while Toinette cleaned the room and, in a chipped liqueur glass begged from Mauricette, a tiny bouquet of flowers was always put in front of it. I was too old to show what I felt or even to say it—and I would not have dared to ask Joss.

With Eliot, as if under a spell, we accepted everything, trusted everything, but when he went to Paris, as he often did, we became suspicious and very critical indeed.

If Mademoiselle Zizi had known that gallery of hard young eyes was watching her I wonder if she would have been different. From morning to night at Les Oeillets we sat in judgment on her, and the judgments were severe. "Well, none of it is *true*," said Hester.

That was not quite fair. In everything there was a grain of truth.

Take her name. Zizi, we knew now from Paul, was a little girl's name, "And she is not a little girl," said Hester. She told lies about Les Oeillets too. "It was my father's house, my grandfather's and great-great-great-grandfather's," Mademoiselle Zizi used to tell the visitors. "The de Presles have lived here since 1731."

"Is it as old as *that*?" asked the visitors.

"It has seen ten wars," said Mademoiselle Zizi. It had been the headquarters of the American Army; the holes in the staircase were from machine-gun bullets; in the cupboard in my room was a stain on the floor; the stain was blood, from an American soldier who had been shot there. On our second day Rita and Rex dug up a skull in the garden.

"Poor house!" Mademoiselle Zizi would say pathetically. "After each war it has healed but now I am the only one left. I never thought to see my home an hotel!" She looked at the conservatory bar with its tables and chairs. "When I was a little girl it was full of carnations, such carnations, with a vine across the roof."

When she said this, if Paul were near, he spat. He beckoned me and showed me a date under the wisteria above the front door. The date said 1885. "M'sieur Presle était boucher," said Paul.

"Un boucher?" I said, disappointed. It did not seem possible that Mademoiselle Zizi was the daughter of a butcher but Paul went on, prodding me with his finger as if he would push the words into me and reluctantly I relayed what he said to Hester. "The butcher bought Les Oeillets as an hotel with money he got from selling bad meat to the soldiers."

The bullet holes were real but when the staircase was painted they were not closed up but picked out again; the stain in the cupboard was made freshly every now and then by Paul with blood from the kitchen; and one day, when a char-à-banc party was coming, he beckoned me out into the garden and showed me what he had in his hand, the skull. It was gruesome, with its eye-sockets and long cheekbones. Paul laughed and made the broken jaw move so that it looked as if it were talking. He had to shut Rita and Rex in the kennel or they would have dug it up at once; he buried it under the urn in the middle flower bed and with it put a piece of raw liver. "Le pourboire," he said and laughed again.

I did not laugh. I was thinking how impressed we had been the first day, how war and death had seemed so close that we had felt almost as Mother had wanted us to feel—ashamed and . . . holy? I thought. Now I felt a fool and I did not like Mademoiselle Zizi or Madame Corbet or Paul; they made Les Oeillets horrid, I thought; but the skull was a man's skull, probably a soldier's, that had been found in the garden. There was a grain of truth.

It was, oddly, Madame Corbet who came best out of our scrutiny, "because she doesn't pretend," said Hester. She was always Madame Corbet, uncompromising, with her black blouse and skirt, stifling shawl, heavy skin, moustache, hard black beady eyes, topknot and all. There was no mistaking Madame Corbet; the sound of her voice, perpetually raised in scolding, haggling, objecting, had at least the sound of honesty; with Mademoiselle Zizi, even more than with the house, nothing was what it seemed.

She had a habit when Eliot was away of leaving the door of her room open and talking across the landing to Madame Corbet in the office while she, Mademoiselle Zizi, was dressing. We could see in and, "Her face is mostly powder," said Hester.

"And do you know," said Vicky in astonishment, "Mademoiselle Zizi's eyelashes take off!" We did not believe that was possible until, spying, we saw it with our own eyes.

"She does that with her bosoms too," said Willmouse.

"Bosoms? Do you call them bosoms?" asked Hester doubtfully.

"I saw them lying across a chair," said Willmouse. He was calm but the rest of us were shocked. "I have made bosoms for Miss Dawn and Dolores," he said. "I never thought of that before."

It was all very odd; Les Oeillets was Mademoiselle Zizi's hotel, yet she asked Madame Corbet for money. "Mais il faut que je m'achète un chemisier"—Hester might have pleaded like that—"un petit chemisier."

I translated that for Hester, who nodded, full of sympathy; she was always on the side of the oppressed. But who was the oppressed one here? "A little blouse."

"Pour lui." Madame Corbet spat out the word. We had long since learned that "lui" was always Eliot.

"I wonder why he chose that hotel." Uncle William wondered that afterwards. "It seems so unsuitable." Then he answered himself as he often did. "But was it? Comfortable, unostentatious, enough foreigners to make him inconspicuous, midway between Paris and the border, and a silly woman who would do anything for him."

"He is ruining the business." Madame Corbet often said that to Mademoiselle Zizi. "Always you tell every client we are full up."

"Not always," said Mademoiselle Zizi.

"And this is the season. All those empty rooms!"

"I do not want to have strangers here with us."

"You are mad."

"Because I do not want to have talk?"

"Talk! The whole town is talking. Someone will report us. In the end we shall lose our star."

I knew what star she meant, the star before Les Oeillets in the guide book. It seemed to be very important but Mademoiselle Zizi only shrugged.

"Ten years," said Madame Corbet in a low, thick voice as if it was choked with anger or tears. "Ten years I could have been a nun but no, I have worked here, to get that star, to pull this hotel up, put myself aside for you. And you will not listen. You throw it all away."

Once we saw Madame Corbet slap Mademoiselle Zizi. The sound of it rang across the hall. It was a slap in the face and

Mademoiselle Zizi stumbled against the desk, holding her cheek with her hand.

It was very quiet in the hall after the slap and we held our breaths; presently there was a new sound, of sobbing, but it was not Mademoiselle Zizi who sobbed; it was Madame Corbet.

Mademoiselle Zizi took her hand down and knelt by Madame Corbet, holding her, rocking her. Little words, in French, broken, reached us, whispered words. "Chérie . . . Jamais, jamais . . . Oubliez ça . . . N'y pensez plus . . . Chérie . . . " We tiptoed away.

It was not often we went away; in fact I do not think we should have left the house at all if we had not been turned out.

That was Eliot's doing. "It's very well for you," I heard Mademoiselle Zizi say to him, "you go off to Paris. I had fifty-eight people for lunch today and these children to see to as well."

"Don't see to them," said Eliot. "Give them some food and turn them out."

"Can I?"

"Of course you can. Children like picnics."

We should have liked it, even preferred it, had it not been for what we missed.

"What did you miss?" asked Uncle William. "A lot of trippers."

"Were they trippers?" asked Hester, dazed. "But . . . we have trippers in Southstone."

The Les Oeillets ones, we were sure, were quite, quite different. They came almost every day. It was the season, "la grande saison," said Mauricette. They came in cars and char-à-bancs. "Then it isn't so queer to visit battlefields," I said. There

were no battlefields now, only fields where corn and grass
grew, and thousands of poppies and marguerites. We saw pictures of them in the guide books. "Do the soldiers come up
in the corn?" asked Hester but, of course, the soldiers were
not there, except those who had been blown to pieces or rot-
ted where they fell, "like the soldier in the garden," said Hester. They were laid in neat rows in the war cemeteries, with
crosses for Christians and stars for Jews. There were pictures
in the guide books of these too. Hester studied them and said,
"I should rather have a star, they are prettier." Paul looked over
her shoulder and made his rude noise. "Mr Stillbotham says
the cemeteries are beautiful, like gardens," Hester reproved
him. "Comme les jardins," she said.

"Jardins!" said Paul, and in English he piped mockingly,
"Be good boy, get killed in war, Papa and Mama come see you
in pretty garden."

There were papas and mamas, sisters, brothers, uncles,
aunts, even a few grandparents; they all seemed to be having
a good time but I could not help thinking of the skull, and the
bullet holes; I wondered what it was like to be buried and not
to be sitting in this pretty satin-papered dining room, eating
the things the visitors ate, hors d'oeuvres and pâté, poulet à
l'estragon, veal and steaks, salads and greengages, and I hoped
I need never be dead.

Most of the visitors were American; we became used to
seeing the far-away place names in the guest book, Illinois,
Wisconsin, California, but there were Canadians, Australians,
people from South Africa, New Zealand, and some, not many,
from England. In the few times we met any of them, on the
landing or on the stairs, they would ask us in French the way

to the lavatory; they took it for granted we were French, which flattered us, and in their efforts to speak to us called the lavatory many strange things. We would listen and ask gravely, "Le pissoir?" and watch their faces as we showed them the Hole.

"But we have modern cloakrooms downstairs!" Mademoiselle Zizi would cry when she heard the chain go. She guessed that it was we who had shown them and made our going out more strict.

Just when things were getting interesting, and at Les Oeillets they were interesting indeed, we were sent away. In the mornings everyone was busy. Madame Corbet would put on a black apron; if Eliot were in Paris Mademoiselle Zizi would attend to the bar but if he were with us Madame Corbet had to do that as well; Mauricette would be in the dining room spreading clean tablecloths, polishing glass and silver; Paul would wipe the little tables under the vine arbour outside and open the umbrellas on the terrace. Monsieur Armand would call him away all the time, and Madame Corbet would call him back. Madame Corbet gave out stores and unlocked the fish tank that stood in the shade of the arbour outside the kitchen and would let Monsieur Armand choose the fish that were swimming in it alive—Hester shuddered when she saw them. "And the snails," cried Hester in agony. We could not bear the snails, "except to eat," said Vicky. They were supposed to come from Burgundy, but Monsieur Armand would take the hotel car, go out in the fields, and gather them in a sack. When he brought them in he would put them in a great tin box full of salt which made them spew and gradually they seasoned themselves ready for eating. It was cruel, but Vicky was right; when they came bubbling in their shells on their

especial silver dishes, with the smell of garlic we were coming
to like, we forgot the box of salt. Vicky had had more of them
than we, but Paul slipped one or two onto our plates when
someone ordered them and showed us how to dig them out
with the small snail fork. We ate the fish from the tank, the
snails . . . "and the chickens," Vicky was to tell Uncle William.
The chickens were cruel too; they were left in a cage so that
they would not walk and spoil the tenderness of their flesh.

As the morning went on Monsieur Armand would grow
more loud and more red; beads of sweat ran along the ends of
his moustache and dripped off though he wiped them with the
end of the cloth he wore tied round his neck. Paul worked like
a machine, and the dining room began to look elegant with
its flowers and tables gleaming with linen and silver. Mauricette shouted to Madame Corbet to come and see, Madame
Corbet shouted back that she was coming. "Un instant," she
would shout. Everyone shouted. Monsieur Armand shouted
to Nicole and Toinette to hurry up and finish the rooms,
Mademoiselle Zizi shouted to Monsieur Armand not to shout,
while Nicole and Toinette shouted downstairs that they could
not do everything, that they had only two arms each and two
legs. Sometimes Mauricette, if she was in a good mood, let us
count out rolls or pleat napkins or snip the brown edges off
the carnations so that they looked like fresh ones; but when
the first people were almost due to come Madame Corbet
would march out of the office and into the kitchen, come back
and set out, on a table in the hall, the packages Paul had made
ready after breakfast. If we were not there she would send him
to fetch us, and would needle looks at us if we did not collect
our picnics at once and go towards the door.

It was strangely ignominious; we had to keep out of sight; Willmouse and I were not allowed into our bedroom because the blood stain was on show and we had to tidy away all our things. Every day it was a feeling of soreness and neglect. "And will they remember to give Joss anything?" asked Hester. "I don't want anything," Joss said each day but I felt she should have been asked. This was the time when we missed Mother most and hated Madame Corbet, Mademoiselle Zizi, Les Oeillets, hated them all. "But not Eliot," said Hester.

"He does not know what it's like," I said. "He isn't here."

Though we were sore, I think now it was those hours by ourselves that kept us sane; they restored us. All the hectic kaleidoscopic bits of this new life, broken up vividly by Paul, came together again in those hours when we had, willy-nilly, to be alone.

I was often quite alone except for Hester, whom I did not count. Vicky slipped back to Monsieur Armand; there was no need to give her luncheon, she had plenty in the kitchen. Willmouse took his package to the cherry tree where his materials were spread out. "I only have time to snatch a sandwich and a cup of coffee," we would hear him murmur and know he was being interviewed by *Vogue* or *Le Jardin des Modes* or *L'Elégance;* Miss Dawn and Dolores were on a diet and ate nothing for lunch except fruit juice, "greengage juice," said Willmouse and we would give him greengages for them and for himself, putting some in our own handkerchiefs to take away.

We were told not to come back until four o'clock and the boundary we were set was the box hedge. On one side lay the house and its happenings, a shifting and changing pattern of

Eliot, Mademoiselle Zizi, Madame Corbet, Paul, Monsieur Armand, Mauricette, the car loads and char-à-bancs of visitors; when we were away from it, it was unreal as the cocktails they all drank or as the top garden with its cut-up flower beds of plants Robert brought in boxes, its gravel, its iron urn, the skull buried every day.

On the wilderness and orchard side was an older, more truthful world; every day, as we passed into it, I caught its older, simpler scents; the smell of box, of mint, syringa, roses, dew on the grass, warm ripe fruit, smells of every summer. There was peace in the overgrown grass walks and heavy bushes, in the long orchard alleys where the greengages ripened in their own time and were neither forced nor pruned; here everything was itself, exactly as it seemed.

When we went through the blue door we were on the margin of the river and here we would sometimes encounter Monsieur Joubert, though soon he would get up and go in to lunch because the light had grown too hard and brilliant. His stool and umbrella were left for the afternoon but I like to think we did not dream of shading ourselves or sitting down. We went to the cove or farther along where the inlet joined the main bank by a plank bridge, and the towing-path ran between the river and the fields. Here and there there was a willow tree, as big as the ones in the garden, its leaves blown silver by the wind; bulrushes grew along the water verges here, great, hot, black-headed, taller than we, and everywhere hung wreaths and cascades of white convolvuli; skiffs were moored to poles dug in the bank and now and again there was a barge tied up. Other barges passed all through the day and we stood still to look at them; some were towing still more barges behind them and whole families lived on board, with washing, hens, firewood, and sometimes a garden planted in pots. When a barge passed we sat down on the bank to let the wash splash up on our bare feet and knees, wetting our scarecrows. There were often peasants working in the cabbages or vines but we did not speak to them or they to us.

Half a kilometre downstream from Les Oeillets was the town; every evening, after goûter, Hester and I would walk there, crossing the bridge by the Giraffe to leave our notes for Mother. Downstream was for the evening, this empty time of lunch and early afternoon belonged upstream, to the country and bare river, as we called this long stretch with its empty banks.

In a way, then, we were bare too; the cocoon of excitement into which we spun ourselves seemed left behind; we went back to being children and that was restful.

A simplicity had descended on us. Coming to France for only a short time, we had few clothes with us; our coats and skirts hung in the wardrobe with our more respectable dresses. We wore our scarecrows which Mother had brought in case we went picnicking, or on a beach and, because we could not be bothered to clean our shoes, we went barefoot.

I do not suppose it occurred to Eliot that we had no money or that we needed any. Madame Corbet had taken Mother's travellers' cheques and cash and our finances had been lifted into a region far over our heads; we could not even read the spiky figures in Madame Corbet's books. "And you are not to bother your mother with anything," said Eliot. "Just write and send your love." Being unable to have anything, mysteriously we did not need anything, except, "How I wish we could bathe at the Plage," Hester said often.

The Plage was the Plage des Saules between Les Oeillets and the bridge where another island made a narrow reach of water that was almost a canal. A white wooden bridge crossed it to the Plage, which was shut off by a railing on which a notice said: "Interdit aux enfants de moins di dix ans qui ne sont pas accompagnés par une grande personne."

The Plage had three swimming enclosures, divided from the main river by painted wooden rods; the green water looked cool and inviting, and there were diving boards and chutes; red and white cabins were Jet for dressing-rooms and there was a kiosk that sold ices and sirops. On hot thirsty days we could read the painted letters on its boards: "Glaces—Fraise, Vanille, Citron, Moka et Chocolat." "Oh well!" said Hester.

There was nowhere else to bathe except the Plage and the cove. The Marne had dangerous currents and at the cove a notice said: "Interdit aux baigneurs qui ne sont pas forts nageurs." Neither of us were the strong swimmers required and all we dared do was to undress in the hotel bathing hut, put on our old salt-stained bathing dresses, and lie in the shallows.

When the clock on the Hôtel de Ville struck one we would come out and open our food. It was a moment to wait for. Paul put up our picnics and he, being on the side of the downtrodden, would filch things we were not supposed to have.

Monsieur Armand told him to put aside yesterday's dinner rolls for us, last night's meat, now cold, sardines and eggs out of the hors d'oeuvres, but Paul would switch the rolls with fresh ones, just carried into the kitchen in the baker's wooden trays, and steal chicken legs, éclairs, or jam tarts and, in the kindness of his heart, pâté, even caviar, which Hester would throw in the river. To us who were used to picnics of hard-boiled eggs, potted meat sandwiches, apples, and milk chocolate, Les Oeillets picnics were banquets; to add to their wonder we were always given bottles of wine and water to drink.

Every day I asked Hester, "Where shall we go?"

"Nowhere," Hester would say, and we would lie in the cove or on the bank and watch the fish, the sun on our backs and heads. In this short time our hair had begun to look bleached, our scarecrows more faded; we watched the fish, or a barge, or a distant peasant family bending and raking, as we listened to the willow leaves or dozed, scarcely talking; there was nothing to listen to but these simple things, no one to look at, no one who was anyone, no questions, and the time would pass until at last from the Hôtel de Ville the clock would strike four and we would sit up and sigh.

The odd part was that, though we chafed at being sent out, when the time came we did not want to go in. Seeing it at a distance and in perspective, I flinched from it. Mademoiselle Zizi, Madame Corbet, Eliot, Paul, they seemed too much but, at least, I thought comfortably, they are nothing to do with us. We are just watching.

Then on the eighth day—it might have been the seventh or the ninth, I had lost count—when we went in and upstairs to see Joss, her shutters were open and she was sitting by her window dressed in a respectable cotton; she had washed her hair and was drying and brushing it over a towel in the sun.

"Are you better?"

"Quite better," said Joss. "Mauricette brought me up some lunch."

"*Mauricette!*"

"She is the maid, isn't she?"

We did not now think of that haughty queen, Mauricette, as a maid.

"Did you ask her?"

"I rang," said Joss simply.

We stared at our sister. Even Vicky seemed to come out of her private shell to take in Joss's unperturbed face with its cool paleness.

"You have washed your hair," I said.

"Yes." She looked at us. "You must wash yours." She did not say what she thought of our dirt and we were silent. At Les Oeillets washing seemed left out of calculations for children, and beside us Joss looked as delicate and fresh as a flower.

Vicky said suddenly, "Mademoiselle Zizi's hair isn't red. They make it red in a shop."

"I know," said Joss.

"You *know*?" Hester and I said that together.

"I knew the first time I saw her," said Joss, leaning forward to look at herself in the looking glass; she had moved to the dressing-table.

"How did you know?"

"Because it was a little bit black at the roots."

"It looks like a bundle," said Vicky. I knew what she meant. Mademoiselle Zizi's hair looked dry and heavy.

Joss did not answer. Watching herself, she picked up her brush and began to brush out her own hair that was soft and impeccably its own black.

CHAPTER VII

That was one of the evenings when Eliot came home. "He likes to get out of the heat and dust of Paris," said Mademoiselle Zizi.

"Ninety kilometres!" said Paul caustically. Ninety kilometres. Eliot had taught us to put them into miles: "Divide by eight, multiply by five." Fifty-five miles was as near as I could get and that certainly seemed a long way to come but, "He comes for her," I said.

"Quatre-vingt dix kilomètres!" said Paul and spat.

When Eliot came, the house was completely changed. Every evening, towards five o'clock, Mademoiselle Zizi dressed herself in one of her pretty dresses; "Not pretty, elegant," corrected Willmouse. She redid her hair, rouged and powdered, put her eyelashes in, and blue-shadowed her eyes. "Then she takes a pencil and draws her eyebrows," said Hester. "How funny to pull them out and have pencil ones instead." Mademoiselle Zizi put scent on her upper lip and behind her ears and—Hester sank her voice" to a whisper, even Hester was

learning that some things should not be openly spoken of—
"she puts scent between her bosoms."

If the telephone rang Mademoiselle Zizi would fly into the
office but usually she would go and wait in the little salon,
which was behind the bar. It too was elegant. We were not
allowed to go into it but could look through the glass panels
of its door; we admired the little room with its pale carpet
that had loops of flowers, its walls that were inlaid with panels
of blue brocade, its table in the middle with paintings in the
wood and the gilt chairs with backs and seats of yellow satin
that were arranged stiffly round the walls.

Mademoiselle Zizi should have been working in the bar
but she sat in the little salon, we knew, because from it she
could watch the courtyard gates and the drive for the first
glimpse of Eliot's car.

No one else had a car like Eliot's. It was a Rolls-Royce, old,
a little battered but its blue and silver length always looked
handsome among the French and American cars. "Why
choose one that stood out?" Uncle William asked that. "Unless
he wanted to stand out," said Uncle William.

Eliot sometimes changed his plans. Then towards dinner
time—and dinner was late at Les Oeillets, often not till ten
o'clock—the waiting would begin to end. Mademoiselle Zizi
would leave the little salon and come slowly back to the bar,
and presently she would follow Madame Corbet into the dining room and to their table by the private screen. Mademoiselle Zizi wilted in her chair, crumbling bread in her fingers,
while Madame Corbet sat upright. On the nights when Eliot
was there he often sat at their table and then, we noticed,
Madame Corbet always ate very quickly, cutting sharply with

her knife—as if she would like to cut Eliot, we thought—not speaking. She would have dark spots of colour in her sallow cheeks and she would always finish and get up while they were still at the second course. Eliot stood up for her as she went but she never gave him a glance, and in a minute we would hear the typewriter keys rattling in the office as if she were typing very fast.

When she and Mademoiselle Zizi were alone, Madame Corbet stayed in the dining room until after everyone had finished. A quiet would be over everything. Monsieur Armand, unless special visitors were there, left the cooking to Paul; Mauricette waited on the tables in her slippers, even the dogs stayed out in the hall, their heads on their paws; no one but Eliot dared give them scraps.

We, of course, had finished long ago; we had our dinner when the staff had theirs but we stayed on at our table, playing cards with old packs from the bar, Racing Demon or Pelmanism or Snap, and we would watch Mademoiselle Zizi's head with its coils of red hair sink lower and lower as she listened to Madame Corbet; then she would go into the bar and begin to drink.

"Oh well. We might as well go out," said Hester.

"Out" meant hanging about in the orchard and the garden, eating greengages, until Paul was free to come out on the steps. Then we sat and smoked with him—even Hester would have a puff. Once Eliot had come home unexpectedly and found us there. We were afraid he might be cross but he only ruffled Hester's hair and said, "You little gossips."

Usually he came for dinner. The dogs would hear his car; they knew long before we did that he was coming and they would stand up, shaking themselves and wagging their great tails. I think we did much the same thing. Hester and Vicky would rush to clasp his legs, while Willmouse stood and smiled, which for him was the equivalent of rushing. "You see," Mademoiselle Zizi said once to Madame Corbet, "see how the children and dogs love him. That is the test of a good man." Madame Corbet sniffed.

With a flounce of her apron, Mauricette would take Eliot's cap and gloves; Monsieur Armand would peer through the kitchen door and start something sizzling on the spit or stove; Paul, if he was there, would mutter under his breath about the extra washing-up and, in the office, Madame Corbet would be still, her topknot craned to watch Mademoiselle Zizi meet Eliot.

On his side there was nothing that anyone might not see. Because of the visitors, if there were any, or for us he would say something quiet, "Bonjour, mademoiselle," or "Ça va?" but she seemed not to care for anyone, the visitors, or us, or Madame Corbet; she would run to him and hang on his arm; it was as if she could not help it, even though, I thought, it annoyed him; when she looked at him, after he had been away, her eyes were so alight with happiness that even I, silly and romantic as I was, thought it would have been better not to let us all see she loved him as much as that. Sometimes Eliot seemed extraordinarily tired; then he had a strained look on his face, a nerve twitching by his mouth. "Well, I expect," said Hester afterwards, "he had often been up all night." Then Mademoiselle Zizi fussed. "You must have a drink," she would say, her eyes searching his face. "I will get you a drink. Have a comfortable chair, not that one. Let Mauricette get you some other shoes." Until he would say, "For God's sake, Zizi!" Then those wide, constantly hurt eyes would fill with tears and her face would quiver. It was surprising a grown person could be so stupid; even I knew that the best thing was to leave him alone until he had been quiet for a while, had one or two drinks, and then say something casual, even rude. That would make him smile and say, "You little tyke!"

That night of Joss's being better there were visitors; a young American with a red sunburned face, three American ladies, and a French colonel with his wife and child; before dinner we all sat at different tables in the bar.

When anyone was speaking French directly to me I could understand, but when they spoke to one another I could not be sure. Now I knew the French family were talking about us, I saw the wife gesticulate admiringly at Willmouse—women always found Willmouse charming while men were doubtful—at Vicky's fall of flaxen hair, at Hester's eyes and curls. These were the family good points and we were used to their being noticed but I thought I heard Eliot say something that surprised me. "'Soeur' is sister, isn't it?" I asked Joss afterwards. "It couldn't be anything else?"

"How could it?" asked Joss.

"Then Eliot said Mother was his sister."

"He couldn't have because she isn't."

"No, but . . . he said he was our guardian."

"I suppose for the moment he is."

"Yes, but . . . He said he always took us to the seaside but this year he had left it too late. He could not get away to see us in England so he brought us here."

"Was this in French?" asked Joss.

"Yes."

"Then you got muddled."

I was sure I had not. Those sentences kept coming back in my mind and, "They were lies," I said.

Eliot talked from our table to the French people, he did not join them. We were all around him; Hester and I were playing Racing Demon at the next table with automatic silent swiftness, our eyes and ears really on him; Willmouse was hunched up in the chair beside him, his nose in his big book. "That boy needs spectacles," Uncle William often said but, "If you get them I won't wear them," Willmouse told Mother. Vicky was on the floor by Eliot's feet where Nebuchadnezzar was grazing in a field fenced with Eliot's matches.

We did not usually cluster round him when he came home but kept a respectful distance, but this evening we were on a different plane. "What is the matter with you?" he had said, looking at us. He looked more carefully and then said, "You are clean."

With Joss up, we had changed for dinner. The scarecrows were on our chairs upstairs, we were in our respectable cottons. That was not all. Usually at this time we went into the dining room to dine before the visitors came in; Paul would get up from the staff table to serve us, probably from a saucepan or a pan, his mouth still full. This evening we waited for Joss. Mademoiselle Zizi was not there, she was in the office with Madame Corbet waiting for a telephone call from Marseille.

At Les Oeillets we had adopted certain places for our own, each one of us had chosen one or two. Willmouse had the bank under the cherry tree, of course, but he also owned the little salon, though he had never been in it, it was his. Hester liked the conservatory and a certain small bed of picotees because its warm close smell reminded her of the carnation Eliot had worn on our first night that seemed now ages ago. Vicky had the vine arbour, perhaps because it was near the kitchen, and she said she liked the bidets—"They are like dear little baths for dolls," said Vicky. I loved the wilderness; it was poetical with its white statues and the white jasmine and, for some reason, I loved the staircase, which was why I so much resented the machine-gun holes.

At that time of day, the sun sinking behind the trees struck through the landing windows and turned the staircase into a funnel of light; even the treads of the stairs seemed barred with gold and, through the round window, came the sound of trills and flutings, the birds singing their evening song in the garden, before it dropped to silence. The staircase might have been Jacob's ladder, stairs to heaven.

I had been looking at it, no, not looking, almost melting into it, Racing Demon forgotten, and had turned my eyes away because of the brightness when I became aware of Eliot's stillness.

"Go on," said Hester, a card ready to slam down, but I did not go on.

Eliot had been going to drink, but his glass was quite still in his hand; the colonel was wrinkling up his eyes, the young American leaning forward. They were all looking.

They were looking at my staircase. Then I saw they were not, or not exactly. They were looking at Joss coming down.

As if those days of sickness and shock had made her clean and delicate she looked pale and . . . pure, I thought, as a snowflake or white blossom, while I was my ordinary brown and pink. She had on the twin of the cotton dress I wore but it was graceful on her; she was wearing the sandals she had bought with her birthday money, white, open-toed, while I wore our clumsy brown school sandals. She seemed to have grown more dignified, taller, and her dress was a little too tight; the shape of her bosoms—forever after I was to think of them as bosoms—showed and the sun gave points of light to the darkness of her newly washed hair.

When I was jealous of Joss Mother used to say, "Jealousy is ugly. It hurts no one but yourself. Don't be jealous," but if one is, how does one help it? It is wrong to be jealous, but . . .

"It isn't wrong," said Eliot when afterwards I asked him this in despair.

"Not wrong to be jealous?" That was against everything I had heard.

"No," said Eliot firmly. "It's what you do with jealousy that can be wrong."

I think I knew that for myself. That night I could have said cruel, unkind things to Joss, wished her any harm; the cards seemed to swim in front of my eyes and I felt bitter and angry as she came quite naturally up to us.

Willmouse went on reading, Hester piled cards on my aces, Vicky grazed Nebuchadnezzar, but Eliot stood up.

That surprised me and made me more bitter than ever. "It's only Joss," I wanted to cry. There was a pause and it dawned upon me that Eliot did not know who she was. "It's only Joss." This time I said it aloud and, as he still looked puzzled, "Joss, the one who was ill."

"One of you?" It was an unflattering disbelief. I had to remember he had only seen her before as a schoolgirl with a big forehead in an ugly hat and, in bed, as a tousled sick child; it was mysterious that these were Joss as well.

"Et c'est votre nièce, cette ravissante jeune personne?" said the colonel from the next table. "Adorable! Adorable!"

Eliot's face looked hot with embarrassment. Did Joss know, I wondered, that she had been called his niece? And ravishing, adorable, I thought, smarting, but she did not seem to have heard and took the chair Eliot pulled out for her and sat down. As he did not speak she said, "I'm better, but you must think we are a most unhealthy family."

She spoke so calmly that, unwilling though I was, admiration filled me. I knew she was shy for there was pink now in her cheeks, and that tell-tale front of her dress moved quickly up and down. Eliot did not answer, which was difficult for Joss. The pink deepened and she tried again, "I hope the children haven't been bothering you."

That was too much. I said loudly, "We don't bother," and Eliot started as if I had . . . wakened him up, I thought.

"Will you have a drink?" he asked Joss.

"Could I have a still lemon?" she said with that false calm.

"He never asked us to have a lemon," whispered Hester as Willmouse was told to go and order one.

"I?" asked Willmouse, deep in his book.

"Yes. You," said Eliot so curtly that Willmouse went.

It was Mademoiselle Zizi, her telephone call finished, who brought the drink. She was puzzled. "Eliot, Willmouse says you want a citron? Is that true?"

As she came Joss stood up. She need not have, under the circumstances, but her schoolgirl habits were strong upon her. She stood up and Mademoiselle Zizi looked at her, as surprised as Eliot had been . . . but, I thought, not at all in the same way.

She and Joss were standing side by side and now I saw Eliot look down; his glance stayed down for a moment as if it were arrested, and I moved my chair to see what he saw. He was looking at their feet. Mademoiselle Zizi was wearing sandals too, open-toed black ones with high heels; they showed her toenails painted deep red but the toes were brown and twisted, thickened with corn marks, the big toes turned inwards with an ugly bump. If I had been Mademoiselle Zizi I should have hidden them and once again her stupidity gave me a pang, for beside her Joss's feet seemed to rest lightly under the white cross straps of her sandals, pretty slim feet, straight-toed, unblemished, the nails pearl-pink. Mademoiselle Zizi had followed Eliot's eyes too. Abruptly she put the lemon down and walked round the table to the other side.

"Merci bien, Mademoiselle," said Joss and hesitated. "I have to say 'good evening,'" she said uncertainly.

Mademoiselle Zizi did not answer at once; she only looked at Joss. Then, "I had not understood," she said.

"Understood?" asked Joss.

"That any of you were . . . so big," said Mademoiselle Zizi.

CHAPTER VIII

Dinner was not comfortable that night. If anyone French came to the hotel, Eliot dined alone, not at the table by the screen; and tonight, all through dinner, his eyes kept coming to Joss, still with that amazed look, and from her table Mademoiselle Zizi's eyes followed his. At last she got up and left the dining room. I do not think he noticed her going.

We, at our table, had long waits because Paul did not come to us at all. He had on the white coat he wore when help was needed in the dining room but he only brought dishes to the service door for Mauricette and took the dirty plates from her. I heard her order him, in angry whispers, to come in and help her but he would not. Joss, of course, did not know it was different; she sat innocently well-mannered and patient but Vicky began to nod with sleep and Willmouse yawned and even fidgeted. It was absurdly late for them but for a long time now their bedtime had been forgotten. I had given up worrying about it after that first day and Joss must have been bemused because she did not say anything. "I never went to bed before eleven, not once," Vicky told Uncle William afterwards.

Hester beckoned to Paul to bring us the dish he was holding in the doorway, but he scowled and turned his back. There was celery soup, stuffed tomatoes, veal with potatoes, flageolet beans served separately as they did here, cheese, and fruit. We had only reached the veal when Mademoiselle Zizi called Eliot from the office. He threw his napkin down impatiently and went out. Soon the visitors finished and left too but Mauricette still walked past us, putting things away instead of bringing our fruit. We, who were familiar, began to be annoyed, but Joss said, "Naturally they have to attend to the more important visitors first."

She seemed not to know that Mauricette was taking it out on us, that Paul was shunning us. How could she? When Mauricette at last planked down our plate of greengages, the cut-glass bowl of water for our fingers, and the clean plates, Joss said, "Merci," as if Mauricette had been normally polite. "Mademoiselle Zizi vous attend dans le bureau," said Mauricette, "si des fois vous auriez fini," she added sarcastically.

Joss looked inquiringly at me; she was not used to Mauricette's quick talking. "Mademoiselle Zizi wants us in the office," I said. "Oh Joss!"

She was a little startled, and we others looked at one another." The table, with us round it, seemed suddenly small and the dining room big and foreign.

"Who gave you permission to change your time for dinner?" asked Mademoiselle Zizi.

Joss looked at me in surprise. "We have been having it when Monsieur Armand and the others have theirs," I explained to her.

"What others?"

"Mauricette, Paul, Toinette, Nicole." I was beginning to regret this childish helter-skelter week; it was partly regret that it was over, our happy obscurity was lost; Joss was dragging us into the limelight.

"Who said you could change?"

Joss turned her eyes on Mademoiselle Zizi. Her voice was still gentle as she asked, "You want us to eat with your servants?"

Mademoiselle Zizi's neck went red. "Mauricette cannot manage with so many in the dining room."

I should have accepted that but Joss answered, "But Cecil says you often have sixty people for luncheon. Tonight we were only fifteen."

"I do not wish"—Mademoiselle Zizi floundered a little—"to have children with adults."

Joss's soft answer came relentlessly. "But Monsieur le Colonel and Madame—I don't know their name—had their little girl with them tonight."

"Do not argue with Mademoiselle Zizi," said Madame Corbet to Joss with such venom that Joss was surprised again.

"I—I'm sorry," said Joss, "but our mother would not like it."

"Your mother left you in my charge," said Mademoiselle Zizi.

Joss could have taken refuge in being small, a child, but, "Could I?" asked Joss afterwards. "I am as big as I am." I suppose she had to be, but I see now that what she said was like a stone thrown into a pool; it spread ripples.

"Your mother left you in my charge," Mademoiselle Zizi said.

"She left us in Mr. Eliot's," said Joss. "Shall we ask him what he thinks?"

I thought Mademoiselle Zizi was going to slap Joss but she controlled herself and, after a moment, "You may have your dinner with the guests," she said, "but I forbid you, absolutely forbid you, to trouble Monsieur Eliot."

After a while Hester and I went to the back steps. We did not want Paul to think we had deserted him but, though he saw us and knew that we knew that he saw us, he did not come. He worked ostentatiously in the kitchen and each time Monsieur Armand passed him he said, "Bougre de gâte-sauce! Marmiton miteux! Espèce de mitrone de merde! Va donc, eh! Ordure!" I knew they were swear words but what they meant I fortunately did not know; and I did not know either why he should be out of temper with Monsieur Armand.

"What *is* the matter with Paul?" asked Hester.

CHAPTER IX

Then came the three days. "I had rather you did not write about those," Joss said after I had put that down.

"I must. They were part of it."

"They were—the only part." When she said that she looked away from me, and neither of us spoke.

The next morning Mademoiselle Zizi had met Eliot in the hall; he had on his linen trousers and dark blue shirt, the canvas shoes that we now knew were espadrilles, his old cap, and was carrying dark glasses. "But you said you were going to Paris," she said and seemed troubled.

He laughed and put his hands on Hester's and Willmouse's heads. "I must see to my family, Zizi." When he saw her face he went to her and, holding her arms, swayed her gently backwards and forwards. "Can't a man have a day or two off?"

In the wilderness he picked a bunch of roses and took Joss and me to see Mother. The doctor, Monsieur le Directeur, met us and, as if we were grown ladies, took us over the hospital. In the men's ward we bowed, as Eliot did, and said, "Bonjour,

Messieurs," in the women's and maternity wards, "Bonjour, mesdames," and felt as if we were royalty.

"A French" hospital is not different from English ones," said Joss, determined to be sophisticated, but I was too uplifted to care if I were sophisticated or not. "*English* hospitals are not called the Hotel of God," I said. "They don't have nuns with their nurses; they were not built in 1304 by the Queen of Philip the Beautiful. There has never been a Philip the Beautiful in England. And the patients don't have wine with their lunch"—we had seen the noonday food trolleys coming up—"and their relations can't come in and out when they like. French hospitals are more interesting and more friendly."

"She is observant, this young Mademoiselle," said Monsieur le Directeur when Eliot had translated for him, and I was flattered.

Eliot talked in the passage with the nun in charge of the private wing while a nurse took us in to see Mother. "For two minutes," said the nun through the open door. I was glad it was only two minutes, for I must admit that seeing Mother dashed the day. The private rooms were blue and white cubicles that seemed shut in another world of hushed quietness. A strange smell hung round Mother—"They had to open her leg again yesterday," Eliot had warned us—and tears ran out from under her lids while she held our hands. I could never have imagined Mother pale but she was yellow-white like wax. We were frightened.

She asked us, "Are you quite . . . all right?" It was a far-away whisper.

"Quite all right." I said it absently for, though I was frightened and full of pity, I could not help listening to Eliot in the passage outside. He can talk to anyone in French or English, I

The town was always gay with its café tables and chairs under striped awnings along the pavements. I had always liked the shop names. "Aux Joyeux Carilons," a happy ring of bells was fitting for toys and games. "A la Fourmi," dresses. Why an ant for dresses? "Ants are industrious," said Eliot. "I expect they sew with little tiny stitches." "Graines potagères, Graines de Fleurs"; I had wondered what that meant. "A seed shop, juggins. Vegetable and flower seeds." "Anne Maria Ferrera. Modes Transformations"; "Crémerie Centrale, en Gros et demi-Gros"; "Les Meubles Tulin"; "J. Binet. Bonneterie Lingerie. Spécialité de Bas."

We had often longed to buy flowers for mother at l'Eglantine: roses, carnations, and glowing spikes of gladioli, and in the hardware shop there was a set of twin cups and saucers in green china lettered "Toi" and "Moi". "Thou and Me," whispered Hester; we thought that touching and meant one day to buy them for Father and Mother. "If we ever have any money," sighed Hester. "And we must take something back for Uncle William. Perhaps one of those pipes with crests and pictures on it or perhaps a vase of those *beautiful* wax flowers."

Now Eliot let us linger at the sweet and cake shop that Joss had not seen; he explained the different kinds of cakes to us: éclairs, rum babas, meringues with crème Chantilly, pears and apples crystallized whole in sugar. He did not make the mistake of offering us any but took us inside to buy a carton of chocolates to take back to Hester and the Littles. There was a rich smell in the shop from the chocolates, and of liqueur from the brandied cherries for which Vieux-Moutiers was famous. There were sugared almonds, marrons glacés, and crystallized violets, rose leaves, and mimosa balls. "But are there no ordinary sweets?" I asked.

thought with a pang. I listened to his easy voice and heard the agitation of pleasure in the little nun's answers, and wondered if a woman could ever be like Eliot; and, if she could, could I be she? I was suddenly more grateful for my punishments at St. Helena's, and to Monsieur Armand and his newspaper lessons, and decided to stop being shy and practise my French on everyone from that day.

"I have been . . . so worried," breathed Mother.

I do not know how Eliot caught that, but he broke off what he was saying and came to her. "You are forbidden to worry," he said. When he was there Mother opened her eyes and smiled at him; she seemed to quieten, not to want to talk any more, and he motioned us to go away. Presently he stood up and came out too, leaving the bunch of roses on the bed.

As we walked back through the town many people greeted him; he was continually stopping and shaking hands with someone. "In France you must always shake hands," he told us. "Watch the children." There were scores of children. If it had been term time, Eliot said, they would have been in black overalls, carrying satchels that were like brief-cases, while the ones from far off would have square luncheon baskets as well; we watched and saw, sure enough, that as soon as the children met anyone they knew they gave their hands. The streets were full of people; there were women in slippers, wearing shawls like Madame Corbet's and carrying heavy shopping bags; there were men in blue overalls, patched and faded, with berets like Monsieur Joubert. There were business men in heavy suits, lorry men and carters, nuns, boys and girls, children all dressed in pinafores, and I said, "Children don't wear pinafores in England."

"You buy those at a grocer's," said Eliot, "but here they have sucettes." Sucettes were lollipops and, "I don't think Mademoiselle Zizi would like us to have those," I said.

We watched while the mademoiselle did the carton up in white paper, tying it with golden, thread and sealing it with a golden seal. It seemed inexpressibly elegant to us. "Don't you get tired of using that word?" asked Eliot when I said this to him, but we did not.

"They don't do boxes up like that in Southstone," said Joss.

"In London they might," said Eliot.

"This isn't London. This is a little town, smaller than Southstone."

"The French understand living," said Eliot, and I longed to be French.

Then he took us to the Giraffe. Dazzled, we sat at one of the small marble-topped tables I had passed so often. The waiter poured wine and water for me but filled up a glass for Joss; Joss tried not to glow but she glowed. When Monsiuer Gérard, the proprietor, came and talked to us she sat very erect, holding the glass of pale golden wine, her eyes going from Monsieur Gérard to Eliot and back again as she tried to keep up with the quick French. I remember that her hair caught the sun again as it struck down through the awning, and from the heat, or perhaps the wine, tiny beads of sweat came out on her forehead and neck. Eliot put out a finger and touched one. "Dew of Joss," he said, and Joss sat oddly still.

"Does it taste of salt?" I asked.

"Sugar and spice," said Eliot and once again his eyes stayed on Joss and he seemed to listen half absently to Monsieur Gérard.

Then we went back to Les Oeillets and on the hall table were our packages laid out.

"What are those?" asked Eliot.

"Our picnics." And I explained to Joss, "We have to go out now."

Eliot looked at the packages, at Joss, and then out to the orchard shimmering green in the sun. A noise of people came from the bar, loud voices and laughter, the sound of glasses, hearty tones, and, "I will have a picnic too," said Eliot.

"A picnic! For you!" asked Madame Corbet.

"For me," said Eliot. Madame Corbet seemed not to know whether to be shocked or pleased but she went to get another package ready.

"What was he thinking of?" asked Uncle William afterwards.

"He wasn't thinking," I said. "Just for once, he forgot to think." I believe now I hit on the truth. I am still haunted by Eliot's voice saying, "Can't a man have a day or two off?"

We went to the cove, "All six of us," said Hester. Willmouse left his sewing and came, Vicky deserted Monsieur Armand though there were going to be oeufs à la neige for lunch. "Alone, with that man!" Uncle William said afterwards of Joss, but they were never alone. We were always with them, a chorus and, though we did not know it then, a guard.

At the blue door we met Monsieur Joubert coming in. When he saw Joss he took off his hat—he changed the beret, when the sun grew hot, for a panama. He smiled and stood back to let us pass, and stood looking after us, the hat in his hand. Joss walked one side of Eliot, her head level with his shoulder. Vicky was on the other, swinging on his hand,

Willmouse and Hester were in front, Hester walking backwards and talking all the time, and I came behind. When I looked back Monsieur Joubert was still gazing thoughtfully after us.

It was a gay picnic. We felt more as if we had escaped than as if we were shut out. After luncheon Vicky fell asleep, her head on Joss's lap; Hester and Willmouse paddled and I lay, as Eliot liked to do, flat, face downwards on the sand. Joss's and Eliot's voices were a low murmur; they seemed to have a great deal to talk about but I was too peaceful to be jealous; everything—and everybody—was at peace.

Then, "Come along, all you lazybones," said Eliot. "I have to go to Soissons. Who would like a drive?"

I sat up and, "In your Rolls-Royce?" breathed Willmouse, coming out of the water.

"Yes. We can look at the cathedral."

In the Rolls-Royce! We looked at one another, excitement spilling out of our faces. "But . . . won't Mademoiselle Zizi mind?" I said.

"Why should she mind?" Eliot's voice had the coldness that only I knew and I was quiet, but none of us went into the house; we washed our faces and hands in the river and left our packages on the back steps.

As we drove along the road to Soissons the stocks were piled in the fields, stocks of dark-coloured corn, darker than in England. In the woods the woodcutters had stacked cut logs to dry. "Think of Having *fires*!" said Hester. The heat was shimmering between the trees and hot air fanned our cheeks. It was unmistakably France, not England; we passed a statue of the Virgin standing above the cornfields, a cart laden with casks of wine, a French military cemetery with a crop of the small wooden crosses we had seen in the guidebooks. At last we drove into Soissons, with the twin towers of its ruined abbey, its thick-walled houses, honey-coloured plaster wash, and wide cathedral square.

Outside the cathedral, "Put something on your heads," said Eliot to Joss and me. "The people like it," but neither of us had anything.

Eliot lent me his handkerchief but there was nothing for Joss; then a woman coming out paused to admire us—it was part of the warm, happy day to be admired; she had been in the cathedral and in her hand had a black lace veil. I had seen women with them in Vieux-Moutiers; they wore them to go into churches and she came up and put it gently over Joss's hair. "Enfin, vous voilà, Mademoiselle," she said and showed Eliot a door in one of the houses opposite where we could bring back the veil.

The meshes of the veil made Joss's hair look even finer and shadowed her face so that it seemed mysterious; her skin looked more ivory than ever and Eliot kept glancing at her. I went and walked by myself, trying not to feel the hot sharpness in my heart.

Inside, the cathedral, with its wide doors opening on the sunlit square, was light, not dim. The long nave was of pale stone cut like huge bricks, the floor was stone too and worn. Why was it so worn?

"This is the old floor. The walls are newer. Soissons cathedral was knocked down in the war. They built it up," said Eliot.

"What! This great thing?"

We had to tilt our heads back to look up at the vaulted roof with its flutings of stone, at the huge rose window in the transept, the long windows below with their amber and red and brilliant blues that sent coloured light down to the floor stones. It was all vast, sealed in quiet. "This great thing," said Eliot softly.

"Il est interdit de circuler dans la cathédrale durant les offices," said notices on the walls, and, "What offices?" we asked, looking round for desks and telephones.

"Divine Offices: Lauds, Vespers, Compline," said Eliot. We still looked blank and he laughed and said, "You little English ignoramuses."

Madame Corbet said often, "The English have no religion," and with Eliot and us as the only English people at Les Oeillets she might have been pardoned for thinking that. "What, no church?" she had asked us our first Sunday, and on the second, "Do you never go to church?"

"At Christmas and at Easter," I told her.

"And when we were christened, of course," said Hester.

"The English have no religion," decided Madame Corbet.

We had not been in a Catholic church; it was interesting, from the massive stone pillars to the gilt Stations of the Cross along the walls. We looked at the rows of chairs. "Do all those people come?" "They come," said Eliot. There was a smell of incense that made us sniff, and we liked the candles that gave a warm light to the small side chapels. "Who puts them there?"

"People," said Eliot. "Watch." People were coming in and out all the time though there was no service. They came and prayed on their own, some of them with beads; some brought flowers and some lit candles. They were not dressed up; some even had shopping bags or tools, one of the women was wearing slippers as if she were at home; indeed, they all seemed comfortably at home. I had not imagined one could feel at home in a church.

In the Chapel of the Resurrection the flowers and candles were white but, to our intense astonishment, the Virgin was black. "Isn't she beautiful?" said Eliot.

Can a black person be beautiful? Such an idea had not occurred to our insular little minds. "Why is she black?"

"She often has a black statue in France," said Eliot.

"The guidebooks say the very first sacred statues were carved from bog oak, which is black," said Joss and she asked, "Would this one be as old as that?"

"I don't know," said Eliot, "but she is very, very old."

"How old?" asked Hester.

"Hundreds of years, I expect," said Eliot, "and she is supposed to be miraculous."

"Miraculous?" Hester was puzzled.

"She can work miracles."

"*Really*?" We all gazed at the statue.

"They say so," said Eliot. "And so thousands and thousands of candles have burnt in front of her and the smoke had turned her even blacker."

"Her cloak is beautiful," said Willmouse in a whisper. It was white brocade with a pattern of blue keys and he put up a finger to touch it. Both she and the Holy Child had on small crowns set with jewels. "Rubies and turquoises," said Eliot.

"Real?" breathed Willmouse and gazed at them, rapt, as Eliot nodded. Hester, who always wanted to test things, held her hand over a candle flame and, sure enough, it made a black mark. Vicky tugged at Joss's arm. "Let me see the rubies," she whispered and Joss lifted her up.

As she held Vicky up to see the crown, Joss's face was lit by the candles so that it was gilded, framed by the black lace. Mother had said Joss was beautiful "just now" but in this moment I knew it was more than that; my sister's beauty was real, for always . . . like a painting, I thought, marked out, and then Eliot's hands gripped my shoulders. They hurt and I craned my head back to look at him and saw what I had guessed from the hardness of his hands; he did not even know he had touched me; he was looking at Joss as Willmouse had looked at the jewels.

A few minutes earlier I should have jerked away, hurt and angry, but now I stood quietly, letting myself be used. Perhaps the Black Virgin had worked another of her small miracles because I did not struggle any more; Joss was beautiful and I was not; she, not I, was marked; Eliot looked at her and did not even notice me and yet I was not jealous. I was sad but it was a Contained, secret sadness and I was not jealous.

When we came out of the cathedral it was good to feel the sun again, warm on our arms and heads. Hester and Willmouse went back with the veil and Eliot made them rehearse what they would say, "Mille remerciements, Madame," and, "Merci pour votre bonté." When they came back he took us all into a pâtisserie for coffee, chocolate, and cakes. Since the shop in Vieux-Moutiers that morning Joss and I had been haunted by visions of babas and meringues, "And those pears," Joss had said longingly, and we took a long while to choose; for Vicky it was the most earnest moment of the day, but Eliot was patient. He ordered chocolate for us and for himself and Joss iced coffee, which came in tall glasses with thick straws and long silver spoons. The pâtisserie was if anything more elegant than the one in Vieux-Moutiers and Joss must have been feeling what I felt, for presently she said to Eliot, "I am sorry about our clothes."

"Your clothes?"

"Yes," said Joss briefly.

"I like your clothes," said Eliot.

"You couldn't possibly." I could tell by the way she said it, her nostrils pinched in, that she was suffering.

"I like them," said Eliot and put his hand over hers on her knee. "I like everything about you."

Again that momentary stillness; then she took her hand away.

The colour of that day was gold but the next was green, for Eliot took us and our picnics to the forest of Compiègne.

All day we wandered and walked in the long avenues and glades of beech trees. In that High summer the forest was intensely green, laced under the trees by green-white cow parsley, with sturdier shapes of bracken and, underfoot, white shamrock-leafed wood sorrel. We found honeysuckle and Hester twined it into wreaths for the Littles. "Willmouse looks like a faun," said Eliot, pointing at Willmouse running in the bracken with his shirt off, the wreath of flowers on his head. Hardly anybody was in the forest. We came upon two empty lakes, reflecting the green and the stretches of blue from the sky where there was not a cloud; white water lilies rocked a little when Hester and Vicky splashed sticks in the water, making ripples; that and the clucking of a disturbed moorhen were the only sounds. "People forget about Compiègne," said Eliot.

When we were tired we got back in the car and drove; the Rolls seemed to go soundlessly down the long avenues and everywhere was the same filtering green, sun rays coming through branches, flickering gently on the ground. We came to a village, grey in the trees, and it had a château, a castle with turrets and walls. "Like the Sleeping Beauty's," said Hester.

I said prettily, "It's a fairy-tale day."

"It isn't. It's true," said Joss. She said it vehemently and vehemence was so unlike Joss that we all looked at her.

"It is true," said Eliot. He drew her arm through his but I could see it was not possible for Joss to walk arm in arm with him and, as soon as she could, she took her arm away.

I do not know what time we ate our luncheon, perhaps three o'clock, and afterwards we lay in the warm grass and slept. Then we met a French family picnicking too; the children were Raoul, Elizabeth who was called Babette, and Jeanne; their names belong forever to that enchanted day. I remember they were playing pat-ball but we taught them rounders, playing England against France. They gave us lemonade and we drank their health before we drove away.

Towards evening we got out of the car and walked again. The sun was lower now and the light slanting down the glades and through the trees was deeper, richer . . . and heavier, I thought. We were heavy too, surfeited with happiness. Vicky dragged her feet, Joss looked pale. "I think we had better have some dinner," said Eliot.

"Dinner?"

"Yes. Do you remember that little restaurant on the lake? Let's go and dine there."

"In a *restaurant*?" Joss and I said together. We had forgotten about trying to be sophisticated.

"Why not?" asked Eliot and Hester promptly exposed us.

"We have never been in a restaurant," she explained, "only in the Violet Tearooms or the Oriental Café."

"Would you like to go in one?"

"But . . . can we?"

"Of course we can," said Eliot.

Joss looked at her watch. "It's nine o'clock!" She sounded a little alarmed.

"All the more reason to dine."

"Won't . . ." I could see Joss did not want to mention Mademoiselle Zizi ". . . they he cross?"

"We shall telephone," said Eliot, but when we came to the chalet restaurant, La Grenouille, its walls painted with frogs, other real frogs sounding from the marsh, there was no telephone. "They will guess," said Eliot. "Come along."

At first we were disappointed. The word "restaurant" for us meant places like the glimpses we had taken into hotel dining rooms as we walked along the promenade at Southstone, the hotels Hester admired. We had thought of waiters, white tablecloths, shaded lights, silver, flowers, napkins cocked into shapes better even than Mauricette made them. La Grenouille was a holiday restaurant, a chalet in a garden where a noticeboard said, "Jeux divers," and there were croquet hoops, seesaws, and swings. The dining room was pitchpine wood, with glassed-in side walls. It was used for shooting parties in the autumn, the patron told us, and on the wooden walls, above the frog paintings, were stuffed heads, a boar, foxes and chamois, while antlers were made into electric lights. The tables had paper tablecloths in green and red plaid—"Paper?" whispered Hester, unwilling to believe it—and the chairs were folding wooden ones. The patron came to meet us in his shirt sleeves and wearing checked cotton trousers and old espadrilles; nor had he shaved. Our eyes examined him disapprovingly while he and Eliot talked. "He can give us soup," said Eliot, "fillet steaks, tarte, and cheese. Will that do?" Distantly, because we did not want to show we were disappointed, we said of course it would do. "Thank you," added Joss and we chorused, "Thank you."

The soup and the yard-long bread from which we broke off pieces as we needed them were good and, as the patron cooked our steaks in front of us and dusk came down, shutting the little glass-sided restaurant into a world of its own, the disappointment went. Eliot gave us vin rosé and the rose-coloured wine, the chaumière flame, the lights were reflected in the windows over and over again, shutting us into a warm, lit world. Eliot talked to the patron and his wife, and we began to talk too; then we were laughing and soon our laughter could have been heard the other side of the lake. Everything made us laugh, for this was better, happier than anything we had imagined.

As we waited for the steaks we read aloud the menu and all the dishes on it, "that are not there," said Eliot and we bantered the patron about that.

"Is andouillette a lark?" I asked.

"That's alouette, duffer. Andouillette is a kind of sausage," said Eliot and translated for the patron. I felt I had been witty as they laughed again. The steaks were cooked with field mushrooms and served with fried potatoes; after them was

a salad and, when the great tarte was brought, its apple filling glazed with apricot jam, even Vicky thought the dinner
complete.

Eliot's face looked calm and happy. He is happy with us, I
thought, and when at last we got up to go it was nearly eleven.
"We shan't get back till twelve o'clock," said Joss.

"Well, what of it?" asked Eliot. He sounded a little defiant
and we looked at one another, our faces scared.

The evening before, when we came back from Soissons,
Mademoiselle Zizi had joined us for drinks; we had the pink
grenadine sirop we liked while she and Eliot drank martinis.
We had told her about the cathedral, the cakes, of all we had
done and seen. She had sat next to Eliot with Willmouse on
the arm of her chair; Joss, on the far side of Eliot, mending
a rent in Vicky's scarecrow, had been so quiet that she was
almost outside the circle; it had all been pleasant and easy but
we guessed it would be different tonight.

Mademoiselle Zizi was waiting when we got in. Eliot had
taken Vicky asleep from the car and, as he carried her in, she
still slept soundly against his shoulder, while his other hand
held up the stumbling Willmouse. The honeysuckle wreaths
were crooked now, Hester and Joss and I had our hands full
of flowers and ferns, our dresses were crumpled, our hair had
leaves in it, and our faces were flushed. "So! You had a good
time!" said Mademoiselle Zizi.

"Thank you, a very good time," said Eliot. Mauricette was
peeping, he beckoned her and gave Vicky into her arms. "Take
Monsieur Willmouse as well," he said. Mauricette would
always do anything for Eliot and she obediently took them.
"Zizi," he said, "give me a drink."

"You look as if you had had a drink already."

"I have had a little vin rosé," said Eliot. "I want a real drink." He looked at her face that had strange pouches under the eyes, patches of red on her cheeks and neck. "So do you."

I did not think she did; she looked as if it was she who had had one already . . . or two or three or half a dozen, I thought. I know now it is children who accept life, grown people cover it up and pretend it is different with drinks and, as Eliot turned her towards the bar, he whispered over his shoulder, "Go up to bed." It was not an order, but said as if in a conspiracy. We silently disappeared and he led Mademoiselle Zizi away.

"But it was spoilt," Hester said and I think she was right. Nothing had that pure happiness again. I wish we had stopped after Compiègne, but the next day Eliot said he must take us to the Caves at Dormans. "And it was very spoilt," said Hester.

It began with trouble over Paul. Eliot had gone down to the Giraffe for cigarettes after breakfast. When he came back he found Paul in his room.

"Stealing?" asked Mademoiselle Zizi, frightened.

"I don't think so," said Eliot. "He was just nosing around, but you can't have that. He must go. At once."

"In the middle of our season?" said Madame Corbet dryly.

"Yes. You can't employ a boy like that."

"Mais, Eliot . . ." pleaded Mademoiselle Zizi, but Eliot would not relent. "I said he must go."

Hester tugged at Joss. "Ask Eliot not to," she said urgently. "Please, Joss. If Paul has to go now he will lose his summer bonus and he will never get his lorry. Ask Eliot, Joss."

Perhaps Joss was not unwilling to try where Mademoiselle Zizi had failed. She went to Eliot and put her hand on his arm, looking up at him, and presently we heard him say, "Very well—if you will come out with me again today."

"Can you spare the time?" said Joss doubtfully.

"Of course I can. We will go to the Caves."

"What Caves?" we said. "It was pronounced "carve," not "cave."

"The champagne cellars. You can't be in the champagne country and not see those."

"Are we in the champagne country?" asked Joss, startled.

"I shall show you," said Eliot.

In our bones we knew it was better not to go—perhaps our bones were getting wiser as they grew stained—but Eliot was queerly determined that morning . . . as obstinate, I thought, as Vicky. When one came to know them it was surprising how childish grown people could be. I think too he did not mean to take the rest of us. He began by trying to get rid of the Littles.

"But I *need* to go," Willmouse pointed out to him. "I must know about champagne."

"We shall leave Vicky then," said Eliot, but he did not know Vicky as we did.

"We are going where we have to walk a long way in the dark," he told her.

"I like the dark," said Vicky.

"You wouldn't like this."

"I would."

"You stay with Monsieur Armand and I will bring you back a doll."

"I don't want a doll. I have Nebuchadnezzar."

"If you come to France," said Eliot, "you must have a French doll."

"All right," said Vicky placidly, but when we were ready in the hall she came downstairs; she had on a respectable cotton, clean socks, her soup-plate hat, and carried Nebuchadnezzar in his basket. "I will help you choose the doll," she said to Eliot and put her hand in his. "And it was odd," said Hester, "if he had not taken Vicky he must have been seen."

For us champagne will always have a ghost; it can never be a wine for feasts but one for mourning. "Because it made the first crack," said Hester.

When we drove in through the important-looking iron and gilded gates at Dormans we had no inkling. It was more magnificent than any place we had seen. There was a lodge by the gates, then a great courtyard laid out with lawns and hot-coloured flowers, red and yellow, and facing the courtyard what looked to us like a palace but Eliot said were packing rooms and offices. As we got out of the car we stopped, not believing our eyes, for wide baskets seemed to be walking slowly past the palace by themselves; "They are bottle baskets on wheels," said Eliot laughing at our faces, "running along their own little railway line."

An entrance with turrets led into the cellars. "But you must not call them cellars," said Eliot. "They are caves, ten miles of galleries, like the Catacombs."

"Tours go over all day long in summer," Eliot had told us and, sure enough, a tourist party was there. It was French but we were allowed to join it and Eliot interpreted for us. The tour of the caves was as quick as going over the cathedral had been slow, and we had no time to say, "Why?" which must have been a relief for him.

We went down into the darkness and coldness of the galleries. "But it is warmer than above ground in winter," said the guide, "because the temperature never changes." First we saw the enormous casks in which the wine waited until it was bottled, then we walked after the French party down the long cellar lanes where the bottles were racked, neck downwards in the pupitres, as the stands were called, and the bottle-twisters moved with their jets of light among the racks, twisting, twisting the bottles with a rattling rhythm that echoed in the vaulted roof.

"Every bottle gets a twist every two days," said Eliot.

"Why?" We did manage to get one in then.

"To bring the sediment down on the cork, and this is an art," said Eliot. "The remueur—bottle-twister—is a devoted person, all his thoughts are for the cuvée he is working on. You see," he said to Hester, "*he* doesn't talk. The whole racking place must be quiet and still, even the currents of air we make as we walk by disturb the wine."

We had not heard of wine being disturbed before and the Littles looked solemn and walked on tiptoe.

We heard pops. "What are they doing?" asked Vicky, enchanted.

"That's where they change the corks," said Eliot. "When the wine is needed the cork is changed." We saw a team of men working together at small machines; they froze the bottle-necks, drew the corks—"Which is what makes the pop!" said Hester, watching—and the sediment with it, smelled the wine, recorked it, muzzled it—"With a tiny wire muzzle," said Hester admiringly—then the bottles were stored—"Upside down again," said Hester—until they were dispatched or used, perhaps years later.

We saw, magnums and jeroboams and half-bottles, and some 1893 champagne draped in the strange webbed fungus that always comes in the caves from the wetness of the chalk. We saw pink champagne—"For the English," said the guide contemptuously and the whole party turned to look at us— and we were shown the rare red wine of the champagne coun- try. Then we came up into the daylight again, to the packing room where women worked at unbelievable speed putting on the gold foil tops, the scarlet seal, the label, and giving each bottle the final wrapping in pink paper.

When we were out in the sunlight again, still surrounded by the party, the guide asked if we would like to visit the museum, in the office opposite. "Would you?" asked Eliot. Hester and I wanted to, but Vicky and Willmouse were tired and as we stood debating a man, dressed as Willmouse hoped to be dressed, in a black coat, striped trousers, white shirt, silver and black tie, and a red carnation, came from the office doorway. Like the women at Soissons cathedral, he had been admiring us.

In Southstone, I thought, if anyone looked at us our spirits immediately curled up in shame and we withered; with Eliot it was suddenly different. It was partly the Rolls, his height, and his clothes, but that did not explain it all; we were the same, dressed the same, yet we were quite different, at ease, confi- dently good-looking and poised.

The man spoke to us in English. "You are English, Monsieur?"

"Yes."

"May I say you have a fine family?"

"We like being called a fine family, don't we?" Eliot asked us and, in this junketing mood, we did.

"Perhaps you would care to take a glass of our champagne with us, Monsieur, you"—I noticed he was looking especially at Joss—"and Mademoiselle and the demoiselles?"

"*Champagne*?" We were dumfounded.

"Would you like to?" asked Eliot.

"Champagne, for *us*?" I could not believe it and even Joss was shaken out of her calm. She put her hand on Eliot's arm and said, "Oh, could we?"

"Can I taste a little, a little?" pleaded Willmouse.

"And I," whispered Hester.

"I don't want champagne, I want a sirop," said Vicky.

"If you would step into our little museum you could look at the pictures until it comes," said the man.

He led us to the door, opened it, then closed it again. From inside we had heard the sound of voices, men's voices speaking French, and footsteps coming near. "A moment," said our man. "They are just coming out. There has been a luncheon in the Directors' room." As we looked impressed he said, "It is the Annual Convocation of Le Brochet de la Marne. That is a fishing club," he explained. "It is a hundred years old and famous. No, not only local, it has members as far away as Paris. Every year they come here for four days—it's a competition, you understand—and on the last day every year the Directors of Dormans entertain them at luncheon. We have some famous members," he said, "doctors, lawyers, artists, even a bishop. This year the guest of honour is what in your country you would call your Sherlock Holmes, one of the greatest detectives in France. If you wait a moment you will see him coming out, Inspector Jules Cailleux."

"Cailleux!" I suppose it was Eliot who said that but it did not sound like Eliot, and I saw he had picked Vicky up and was holding her in front of him on his arm.

"Put me down!" She was mortally offended. She slapped Eliot but he did not put her down.

"We have forgotten your doll," he said and looked at his watch. "Nous vous remercions infiniment, Monsieur, mais nous n'avons vraiment pas le temps d'attendre. Merci mille fois," and—what was he saying?—"I had forgotten. I have an appointment in Reims."

"Mais, Monsieur . . ."

"Je regrette . . ." And he turned to us. "Come along."

"But . . ."

"Eliot!"

"You said . . ."

"Come *along!*" Eliot's voice was as I had heard it once before, cold and clipped. "Come, if you don't want to walk home. Encore mille fois merci," he said again to the man. "Un autre jour."

He went towards the car, holding Vicky who hid his face from us. We were following, amazed, when a group of men came out of the door, three of them dressed like our man, the rest in suits or flannels and tweed jackets; there were two priests and, in the middle, a little man in a suit of mixed sand-and-olive-coloured cloth that went well with his sand-coloured hair and clipped moustache. "That must be the Inspector—did he say Cailleux?" asked Joss. The men's faces were red and they all looked jovial but, great detective or not, we were given no time to look. Eliot had started the Rolls and we had to run across the courtyard and scramble in, even Joss. It was the first time he had treated her in this undignified way—he might have been Uncle William—and her cheeks looked as if they burned.

He drove swiftly round the courtyard and through the gates and, before the men had left the office steps, we were out on the road and speeding down it.

We drove in dead silence until at last Hester spoke. "This is the road to Soissons, Eliot."

"I know."

"You said you had an appointment in Reims."

"I know."

After a moment Hester asked, "Do you tell lies, Eliot?"

"Yes."

He drove fast into Soissons and stopped at a toyshop, got out, and helped Vicky from the back seat; he glanced at Joss and said, "Cecil, you come."

In the shop he was not as he usually was with people. "Une poupée? Mais oui, Monsieur. Voulez-vous une belle petite poupée ou une originale?" the shop girl asked. I did not know what "une originale" meant, but Eliot did not answer and I had to say, "Une belle petite poupée, that means a pretty little doll," I told Vicky.

Vicky took a long while to choose but, when we were back with the others and heading for Vieux-Moutiers, the silence was still unbroken.

At last Eliot stopped the car. "I'm sorry I had to do that," he said.

"Then why did you?" asked Joss.

"I had a reason," said Eliot, "that you would not understand."

"Then you can't expect us to understand, can you?" asked Joss. Her voice was cold but it trembled a little.

"All right. I tell lies," said Eliot violently. It was the first time he had come up against a family opinion. "I tell lies and so do you and you and you, all of you."

"For you to tell them is different," said Hester.

"I didn't ask to be a hero."

"They mean you are grown up," said Joss coldly.

"I see," said Eliot. "You expect yourselves to be comfortably riddled with faults . . ."

"We are."

". . . and you think you will lose them when you grow up."

"I hope so," I said firmly.

"You poor little fools!"

Joss put her hand on Eliot's knee. "Eliot, what has made you so unhappy?"

He looked down at her hand and I shall always remember his answer. "What has made you so unhappy?" Joss asked and he answered, "Being perfectly happy for two days."

After a moment he turned to look at us in the back seat. "Has none of you ever tasted champagne?"

"Don't be *silly*," said Joss, exasperated. "How could we?" And I said sorrowfully, "We have never even seen it."

"It is not as exciting as all that," said Eliot. "You soon get tired of it." Silence. "I suppose, to you, that is another silly thing to say."

"Yes."

He did not say anything more but started the car. When we got back to the hotel, we separated; it seemed by mutual consent.

There were roses on our table that night. Usually ours was the only one without flowers. Nobody else was dining but

Monsieur Joubert and Eliot; Madame Corbet's and Mademoiselle Zizi's places had not been used. Besides the roses we had
a clean starched cloth—often ours was left on dirty—clean
napkins made into cocked hats, and by each place was a new
kind of glass, high, with a three-inch stem, cut into patterns.
"What are these?" we asked.

"Flutes de champagne," said Mauricette and laughed.

"Glasses for drinking champagne," said Monsieur Joubert in
careful English. He had never spoken to us before except to say
"Bonjour." Now he was as interested as Mauricette. "They have
a hollow stem and keep the wine to sparkle," he explained.

Mauricette served our soup. She was friendly that night
and did not slam things down on the table or lean across us.
After the soup there was chicken, not the perpetual veal and
flageolets. Then Mauricette, with a smile at the corners of her
mouth, brought in one of the silver wine buckets we had often
helped to fill with ice; she stood it by our table. In it was a dark
green gold-topped bottle. It might have been one of those we
had seen that day. Eliot left his table, came to ours, and drew
the cork, making us jump. It was the same popping we had
heard at Dormans but it sounded louder in the dining room.
Then Mauricette wrapped the bottle in a napkin, carried it to
Eliot's table, and poured a little into his glass and gave it to
him to taste. He sipped it and nodded. For one moment we
had thought it all might be for him, but she filled Joss's glass,
and went round the table. After Hester, she hesitated, but Eliot
said, "Monsieur Willmouse will take a little. Bring a grenadine
for Mademoiselle Vicky."

We sat in amazed silence, looking at the glasses and the
pale sparkling wine. I think our eyes must have been quite

round, our faces awed, but I admired Joss. No matter how moved, she did not lose her manners. She got up, went to the bucket, reverently lifted the bottle from the ice, copied Mauricette by wrapping it in a napkin, took it to Eliot, and filled his glass up. "May I offer some to Monsieur Joubert?" she asked.

"It's your wine," said Eliot. "Say, 'Vous prendrez bien un verre, Monsieur?'"

She took it to Monsieur Joubert. "Vous prendrez bien un verre, Monsieur?" Mauricette ran with a glass and Joss poured. "Thank you, Mademoiselle Hebe," said Monsieur Joubert.

When Joss was back in her place he lifted his glass and called, "Santé!"

"Santé."

"Santé."

"Santé."

"Santé."

"Santé."

Willmouse was white, Hester approached her lips as if she were afraid champagne might bite, Joss looked over her glass at Eliot and quickly lowered her lids, and we drank. "It goes up your nose," said Willmouse. "I like it going up my nose."

"Monsieur Eliot," called Monsieur Joubert, "you must take the bouchon—the cork—wet it and touch it behind Mademoiselle's ears." And to Joss, "Always with the first bottle of champagne you taste that must be done."

Eliot came over to us. Mauricette gave him the cork, he wetted it, and we watched, as in a ritual, while he lifted Joss's hair and touched it behind her ear. I do not know why but we all clapped. "Now you must keep it forever," said Monsieur Joubert to Joss.

"Eliot! *E-liot!*"

Mademoiselle Zizi's voice rang through the hall. The next moment she appeared in the dining room. "Eliot!"

I thought that, quite deliberately, he touched the cork to Joss's other ear before he answered, "I am here, Zizi."

"Irène says you ordered champagne, Dormans—for those children."

"Yes."

"Are you mad?"

"It was for a reason, Zizi."

Had Mademoiselle Zizi forgotten her rouge? She was curiously white; her eyes had dark, purple-coloured stains under them as if she had spilled the eye shadow, only it was darker than that. "I know your reason!" said Mademoiselle Zizi.

Those haunted-looking eyes took in the table, the roses, the chicken. "Who said you could do this?"

"Pauv' p'tits choux!" said Mauricette. "Y sont si mignons, ces enfants." She had often called us the reverse of cabbages or sweet. "Armand et moi leur avons préparé une petite surprise."

"With my things?"

Joss got up. She did what she thought was the best thing. Taking Vicky's flute de champagne from where it stood unused beside the glass of grenadine, she filled it from the bottle and brought it to Mademoiselle Zizi. "Mademoiselle, vous voudrez bien prendre un verre?"

I thought she would not but Mademoiselle Zizi took the glass. Her eyes turned from Eliot to Joss and back to Eliot. "Santé," said Eliot pleasantly.

Mademoiselle Zizi went even whiter; her mouth made an ugly grimace, and she threw the champagne back at Joss.

We knew from newspapers and books that grown people quarrelled but we had never heard them.

After Mademoiselle Zizi had thrown the champagne no one moved or spoke though Mauricette gave a loud gasp; the glass had fallen with a tinkling crash and the tinkle seemed to go on and on. Then Monsieur Joubert got to his feet and walked out of the dining room and Vicky began to cry. "I want Mother. I want Mother," she wailed. Joss's dress was wet with champagne, it trickled down the front of her skirt; she shook her hair back as if she were dazed, then ran out of the room and through the hall. We heard the terrace door bang, and Eliot said to Mademoiselle Zizi, "I want to see you alone."

They did not wait to reach the office before they began; their angry loud voices rang through the hall. They spoke English when they remembered because of Mauricette and the rest who were listening with all their ears, but they kept breaking into French.

"I should never have let them be there at dinner," cried Mademoiselle Zizi. "That girl!"

"She was quite right," said Eliot. "The small ones could eat with the servants, but she and Cecil are big."

"Of course you take her part."

"I don't."

"You do. For three days I have scarcely seen you."

"For Christ's sake, Zizi! I happened to have a little time and amused the poor brats."

"Brats. Qu'est-ce que c'est "brats"?"

"Children, then."

"You don't think of them as children."

"Don't be ridiculous."

"Ridiculous! For three days . . ." Mademoiselle Zizi was crying.

"*Don't keep on saying that!*" Then Eliot's voice altered. "Zizi, you're not jealous of a little girl?"

"First she is big, then she is little. Remarkable!" That was Madame Corbet, who had come out of the office.

"Is it too much to ask," said Eliot, his voice like ice again, "that we might occasionally talk without Irène?"

"And why may I not remain?"

"Because this is not your business."

"Zizi is my business. I gave up my vocation to look after her."

"Then it was not a vocation."

"Irène, please go." That was Mademoiselle Zizi.

"And leave him to talk you down?"

"Go! Go! Go!" Mademoiselle Zizi's voice was a scream.

"Let *us* go," said Hester and her voice quivered. "Let's go in the garden and get some greengages," but before we could move Madame Corbet came through the dining room. Her neck was patched with crimson, her topknot shook, and the bobbles on her shawl danced up and down. "Ah, le vaurien! Canaille! Fripouille!" said Madame Corbet as she passed. We shrank down in our chairs.

"Eliot, écoute. Ecoute-moi . . ." Mademoiselle Zizi's voice was soft and I guessed she had gone close to Eliot. I stood up to see and yes, she had; she was standing in front of him pleading. "It is too much responsibility, Eliot. Please! Please let us send for this uncle and get them away."

"Dear Zizi, because of a child . . ."

"She isn't a child."

"Of course she is, to me—to us."

"I saw you look at her."

"She happens to be pretty."

Mademoiselle Zizi shook her head. "You looked at her because you like her."

"Don't be absurd."

"Then send for the uncle."

"Zizi." Eliot had taken her hands. "I gave my word, besides . . ." I had the feeling he was choosing the words very carefully. "I can't have the uncle, an Englishman, here now."

"Because he is English?" She sounded scornful.

"I explained to you, Zizi. I can't have talk yet."

"But a man in Southstone. That is in Sussex, it is far away from London."

"Not so far. I can't afford to risk it."

"But if I don't mind."

"I mind for you, and if there were talk it might spoil everything."

"But Sussex and London," pleaded Mademoiselle Zizi.

I did not know what they were talking of. I could have told them that Uncle William never went to London but Eliot sounded as if he were . . . making excuses, I thought. He said now, "You never know."

"N-no," said Mademoiselle Zizi slowly and . . . she is coming to heel, I thought.

"Zizi, promise. Promise me you won't do anything."

"Irène says . . ."

"You know Irène would do anything to separate us. Promise." Without looking I knew he had put his arm round Mademoiselle Zizi. I looked at the floor, the blood thrummed in my ears, and my little lemons throbbed. "Zizi."

"Let's go out," whispered Mademoiselle Zizi. "Let's go away from here. Somewhere. Anywhere."

"But why?"

"Because."

"Because?"

"I can't bear it," cried Mademoiselle Zizi. "The house, Irène, them. All of them."

"Get a coat then," said Eliot. He sounded as if he had given up. Why should he sound like that when it was Mademoiselle Zizi who had been defeated? I tiptoed out into the hall. He was there alone but Mademoiselle Zizi was only fetching her coat; and she soon came back. He said as if he were very tired, "Come through the garden. We will go to the Giraffe."

As they reached the glass door it opened and Joss stood there. Behind her the garden was twilit now; she must have been alone in the dusk . . . in the orchard, I thought, looking at her drenched sandals; her feet and the hem of her dress were soaked, and it was only in the orchard that the dew lay like that. I did not think Joss knew where she had been. Her eyes still looked shocked.

For a moment Mademoiselle Zizi and Eliot stopped. Then Mademoiselle Zizi walked past, her head high.

Joss's eyes went to Eliot. There was no appeal in them, she simply looked. There was a pause, like a breath. Then Eliot squared his shoulders as if he had made up his mind. He went after Mademoiselle Zizi and passed Joss as if she were not there.

CHAPTER X

When someone has been slapped in the face it is polite not to look at them. I went to a table in the bar, picked up a magazine, and turned the pages over while Hester quietly gathered Vicky and Willmouse and took them to bed; I heard them go one after the other in the Hole, then the bedroom doors shut.

The house had never seemed so big. I could hear Madame Corbet scolding Paul; I knew it was Paul because he did not answer as Mauricette did, then I remembered that Mauricette was not there. She had gone to the cinema with Monsieur Armand; soon after the quarrel began we had seen them cross the courtyard and go out arm in arm.

Madame Corbet came from the kitchen and went into the office. I heard her lock up, take the keys, and go out. Would she go to the Giraffe and spy on the others or to the convent which was where Paul said she went, though the convent would hardly be open at this hour? I could not guess but, soon after, all the lights went off. That was one of Madame Corbet's economies; if she wanted to go out and the house was empty of people—we and Paul did not count as people—she would turn off the electricity at the main; she would be back, the lights suitably burning, before Mademoiselle Zizi and Eliot came in.

Though it was only dusk outside the house was immediately dark which made it more desolate. At other times when Madame Corbet had done this Hester and I had been in the garden with Paul, "talking gossip," said Joss scornfully but, quite often, "Not gossip, dreams," I could have said. We talked about what we should do when we were grown; I was to be a writer or a nun, a nun as Madame Corbet had wanted to be; Hester thought she might keep a teashop or an hotel like Mademoiselle Zizi; Paul talked about his lorries. "If I stay the summer," he said, "I shall get the bonus," and he told us again how, at the end of the season, Madame Corbet shared out the tips. "It makes a lot," said Paul; he had seen a good second-hand Berliet at the garage; but now Joss and I were inside; even the dogs were away, they had gone with Eliot and Mademoiselle Zizi, and the house was eerie; it seemed to creak with invisible footsteps, a breeze in the garden sounded like rustling, a curtain flapped. There was a waxing moon and the early moonlight, mixed with dusk, fell in at the windows and made the light more eerie still. Joss must have felt it for she came and sat at the table by me. I could just see the pale oval of her face, the whiteness of her arms.

"Shall we go to bed?" I asked.

"I . . . can't." There was a pause. Our voices in the emptiness seemed small, then, "They have even kept our passports," said Joss.

"Our passports?" I asked.

"Yes. How dared they!"

"But . . . what should they have done?"

"They are ours," said Joss fiercely.

"But why do you want them?"

"I'm going home," she snapped, "and one can't travel without them."

"But . . ." Every sentence I said seemed to begin with "but." "But how can you go?"

"By myself if I must." And she thrust at me, "You were quite happy without me when I was ill. You were happier."

The way in which she said it made it a guilty thing to have been but I had to admit it. "But it is far more interesting now," I blurted out.

"You call it interesting!"

"Yes. Oh Joss! Don't, don't spoil it."

"*Spoil* it!" She bent her head.

"I know it is sometimes difficult . . ." I began.

"Difficult!" All she seemed able to do was echo my words, spitting them out as if they tasted bitter.

"Yes, I know, but we are *alive*," I argued. "Think how alive we are. It isn't like Southstone where we just went on and on and nothing ever happened. Here I can feel us living. Don't you feel as if you were being stretched?"

"It hurts to be stretched," said Joss.

There was a flapping sound that was oddly cheerful, not the flapping curtain but a flap of slippers, and a glimmer of light appeared that grew larger. Joss raised her head as Paul came through the kitchen doorway carrying two lighted candles in bottles. "Vieille guenon!" he said of Madame Corbet. "Came!" The bad words sounded matter-of-fact and cheerful too. Paul put the bottles down on our table. "V'là ce que j'ai trouvé!" he said, felt in his pocket, and brought out the champagne cork. He put it beside Joss.

"Merci," said Joss dully.

"Vous n'en voulez-pas?"

Joss shook her head. "It doesn't seem very lucky," she said and, laboriously, "Pas bonne chance."

"C'est la vie," said Paul without rancour. "Des gens." People! I thought, and winced.

"Psst!" Paul spat the people out on the floor. Joss did not even flinch. In fact, she looked better. Perhaps it was the chili in the elephant's eye. Father had told us about that; in India when an elephant has a wound that hurts so that the pain cannot be borne, the mahout squirts chili juice into its eye for the smarting to distract it.

I guessed that Joss would have liked to spit too; then the anger faded; she rolled the cork forlornly on the table.

Paul looked at it and her, then he whispered to me. "He kept the champagne," I told Joss.

"I don't want it."

"Le champagne c'est toujours du champagne," said Paul. He added that he was not going to let that she-cat have it.

"The she-cat is Mauricette," I explained to Joss.

"What can we do with it?" asked Joss.

"We could . . . drink it," I said timidly.

"Out of other people's glasses!"

"Only ours. Monsieur Joubert drank his. Ours and . . . Eliot's." Joss turned her head away.

Paul came back with a round tray. He had tactfully poured all the glassfuls back into the bottle so that no one could know which was which. There were two clean glasses. "Where is yours?" and I asked clumsily, "Et pour vous?"

A pleased look came into his face but he looked at Joss. "Certainement," said Joss.

He fetched another glass and I filled it.

"Ça fait du bien par où ça passe," said Paul, drinking. His eyes seemed eager.

"Santé!" I said, but Paul would not drink to that.

He spat again, then lifted his glass. "Encore un que les salauds n'auront pas. Qu'ils aillent au diable, les cassepieds."

"Les cassepieds!" I said.

"Les cassepieds!" said Joss, her eyes dark.

We drank. I tried not to grimace at the strange feeling in my nose but my eyelids flickered so that Paul laughed. Joss managed to hide everything but one long shudder.

"Vous vous y ferez vite," said Paul, but I did not think we should soon get used to it. He and Joss finished the bottle, then he looked at the empty glasses and asked, "Encore un coup, hein?"

"Encore?" Paul tapped the bottle and pretended he was opening another. "But it's all locked up," I said.

"Si," said Paul mockingly.

Joss thought he had not understood. "Madame Corbet a emporté—has taken the keys—les clefs," she said.

"Si," said Paul and laughed. Then he flapped across the hall and went into Mademoiselle Zizi's room. In a moment he was back, holding up a bunch of keys.

"Zizi, where are your keys? You had better give them to me." How many times had I heard Madame Corbet say that and, "You are not fit to have them." It seemed Madame Corbet was right.

Paul turned towards the kitchen door. Behind it stone steps went down to the cellar.

"But, Paul—"

Joss cut across me. "Go on," said Joss. "Allez-y." She was not despairing now but sitting up straight. "Go on," she said to Paul, and I knew that the hurt was really angry now. That made me afraid; when Joss was angry she did not care what she did.

"Joss. He shouldn't—"

"Shut up," said Joss.

Paul came back with two tall bottles. "Vous en boirez pas du comme ça à l'étranger," he said. "C'est moi qui vous le dis."

I was proud that I could understand him when Joss could not. "You won't drink this away—outside France."

"Why?" asked Joss. "What is it? Qu'est-ce que c'est?"

"Champagne nature." And seeing we did not understand he said, "Blanc de blanc."

When I think of that evening it seems to run together into that name. "Blanc de blanc." It sounded like the name of a fairy prince—I think the bubbles in the champagne were mounting to my head—blanc de blanc de blanc de blanc . . .

"We mustn't drink it," I said but the words seemed to burst in the air and disappear.

"We drank the other," said Joss.

"Our wine . . . given to us." Now I seemed to have lost some words.

"Shut up."

Paul caught that. "Shut up," he said amiably to me and poured the wine. Joss lifted her glass to me and drank; she emptied the glass straight off. "Mazette!" said Paul in admiration. He filled it again and she laid her hand on his. "Thank you, Paul," she said. "It was s-sweet of you to get this for us." She had drunk too quickly. The "s-sweet" was a tiny hiccup, but it was not that that sobered me. It was Paul's face. Paul had not understood what she said, but his face had flooded with crimson and that pleased look was in his eyes.

"Joss, don't. He will think you mean it."

"W-what if he does?" She leaned towards Paul and said, "You give cigarettes to Cecil. Why not to me?"

"Cigarette?" Paul sounded dazed but he brought out his packet. Joss took one and he tossed her the matches. It was not that he meant to be rude but he did not know how to treat girls. Joss tried to light the cigarette but the smoke got into her eyes. Paul laughed at her and, taking the cigarette, lit it himself, then he put it into her lips.

For some reason I did not like to see that. "Joss, don't."

"Why not?"

I would not say why not, I said instead, "You will hurt him."

Her eyes narrowed into small glints. "I am g-going to hurt him." This time the hiccup was loud.

"You are getting drunk," I said disagreeably.

"I want to. I am going to get d-drunk." She lifted her glass. "I am g-going to do all the d-disgusting things they do." She drank the wine off and held out her glass while I was doubtfully sipping mine. I do not know how many Paul had had but when he had poured for her the bottle of blanc de blanc was empty. "L'autre," commanded Joss.

Paul picked up the other and showed it to me. "Bouzy Rouge," he said.

"Bouzy? Bouzy. Bouzy." Joss started to laugh and the laugh turned into giggles like the bubbles coming up. "C-Cecil.

B-Bouzy!" but I was still with blanc de blanc. It was a moun-
tain, a pudding, shoe polish, a white poodle.

"Boozy," said Joss.

"Blanc de blanc de blanc."

Paul looked at us gravely. He was swaying a little as he
stood and said solemnly, "Il faut se mettre à genoux pour
déguster celui-là."

I did not understand. "On our knees to drink this? Why?"

He put his hands together and rolled up his eyes.

I collapsed into more giggles, Joss giggled too. "What does
Boozy say?"

"He says we should . . . pray."

"Let's pray." She put her hands together, but I took violent
exception to that. "Joss, you are not to. You . . . *are . . . not . . .
to!*" I banged the table with the empty bottle.

"P-pious p-prig!"

"N-not a p-prig!" and I burst into tears. Joss looked as if
she might cry too. She put her arm round my neck. "Don't,"
she begged. "Don't!"

"Then you don't," I said, still angry, and she pulled away,
offended. "Cry then," she said. "Howl. I don't c-care. Tell Paul
to open the wine."

Paul was having difficulty with the corkscrew. He located
the cork but as soon as he tried to spiral the screw in, it slipped
sideways. Now he tried again and seared his thumb. "Aie!
Merde!" said Paul. "Hit it," said Joss, "tapez dessus," and he hit
the bottle against one of the console tables. The neck smashed
off on the floor with a gush of red wine that spattered his
apron and hand. There was an ugly great gash across the table.

I was horrified. "Paul! *Paul!*"

He swore at me with his new word, "Shut up!" and poured the wine.

"I don't want any," I said but he picked up my glass, drank the white, and filled it with the red. It seemed to my bleared eyes that the whole hall was spread with red wine, the glasses were red and the pool on the floor. Paul's and Joss's heads seemed to come nearer and go away again as did the candle flames in the bottles. When I looked at the walls they moved inwards a little, while the stairs went sideways. It was no longer blanc de blanc, that happy time; the red was terrible, and I began to cry again.

Joss had drunk her glass already. I do not know why she was not sick. "Another cigarette. Encore une Gauloise," she said.

Paul looked at her. His eyes seemed to squint so that he looked hideous and he said, "Viens la prendre."

He was sitting back from the table, his knees apart, his apron dangling between them, a cigarette stuck to his lower lip. Now he pulled open his shirt and showed where the cigarettes were crumpled inside. "Viens-y," he said Joss went pale and stood up uncertainly.

I knew what he would do. I had seen him with Mauricette too often. Mauricette could look after herself but, "Joss you are not to!" I screamed. "You are not to!" I pushed her down and screamed at Paul, "Ne la touchez pas!"

He turned on me and ordered me to bed. "Toi, va faire dodo! Au pieu!"

"I won't. Joss! Joss!"

Paul picked up the bottle. I do not know what would have happened if Joss had not settled it herself. She had been sitting where I had pushed her; now, quite softly, with a sigh, she fell forward on the table, knocking over my untouched glass. Her head rolled a little, her hair tumbled forward into the wine and began to soak it up.

We heard footsteps. The garden door opened, Monsieur Joubert and Mademoiselle Zizi came in and stopped, with Eliot close behind them. At the same moment the lights went on and there was a scurry of steps in the kitchen passage; Madame Corbet had stayed too late and the others had beaten her; she came running in breathless and stopped too. "Grands Dieux!" said Madame Corbet. The others said nothing, they simply stood.

It must have looked an orgy with the bottles and glasses, the candles burned down in the bottles, the wine on the table, the cigarette ends where we had thrown them down on the floor with more wine and broken glass. "Grands Dieux!" said Madame Corbet again.

Then I saw the rat in Paul. "C'est pas moi! C'est pas moi!" His voice was shrill with fear. "C'est elle"—he pointed at Joss— "elle et Mademoiselle Cecil. Elles m'ont forcé!"

"La ferme!" said Eliot, which was the rudest way I had heard of saying "shut up."

Mademoiselle Zizi had stayed in the doorway; it was as if she kept her skirts held back. Eliot crossed at once to Joss but before he reached her Monsieur Joubert came up behind and stood with his hands on her chair. It was as if he kept Eliot off. Monsieur Joubert bent and straightened Joss up but she could not sit; her head fell forward again. "She is drunk," said Monsieur Joubert to Eliot as if it were an accusation, and he said, in English too, "I do not know what has been going on here but it is not good." He was not looking at us but at Eliot and Mademoiselle Zizi.

"*Good!*" Mademoiselle Zizi was defensive. "To be drunk at their age! On my wine!"

"And look at the table!" cried Madame Corbet.

"Ma petite table! My little table! Ah!" Mademoiselle Zizi's voice was agonized.

Madame Corbet darted forward and picked up the bottles. "Zizi! The Villers Marmery and Bouzy Rouge!"

Paul had been picking up the broken glass. Now he rolled it in his apron and slipped adroitly through the kitchen door. Joss was insensible, there was only I, Cecil, to face them. I was standing unsteadily where I had risen by the table and Madame Corbet turned on me and slapped my cheeks. "Petite canaille . . . J'm'en vais te flanquer une correction. Drôlesse! Oh! Cette petite crapule!"

"Stop that, Irène," said Elliot. "Stop. Hush!" he said more loudly as the stream of names went on.

"Hush! And who is to pay for it?"

"You can put it on my bill," said Monsieur Joubert and there was silence. He bent and picked Joss up. "Mademoiselle Cecil, can you walk upstairs to your room?"

My ears were singing with Madame Corbet's slaps but I managed to leave the table and zigzag to the stairs; there the banister rail came unexpectedly into my hand. Monsieur Joubert followed, carrying Joss.

"Let me take her," said Eliot.

"I think you have done enough," said Monsieur Joubert. He carried Joss up. I followed, missing some steps but holding by the banister rail. Eliot was left standing at the foot of the stairs.

CHAPTER XI

I f this is how grown people feel," said Joss, "they are even worse pigs than I thought."

I said, perhaps tactlessly, "They know when to stop."

"Do they!" said Joss. "Look at Mademoiselle Zizi," but I had to be fair.

"Of all the grown-ups she is the only one who doesn't seem to know," and I sighed. "I suppose one has to learn even to drink."

I did not remember getting into bed but I had waked to find myself under the clothes though dressed. "Dressed in bed!" said Willmouse. "Cecil, *what* have you been doing?" It was not often Willmouse asked questions and, when he had seen how unwell I was, he had slipped on his vest and shorts, brushed his hair, and gone out. I think he kept Hester and Vicky away.

When I had gone in to Joss she too was in bed, the covers tucked carefully round her, her sandals placed neatly side by side on the rug, but she also was dressed. I felt so miserable that I woke her and she was cross. Then, sitting up, she had taken in where she was, her crumpled dress, the smell on her hair, and she gave a sound like a moan and shut her eyes.

We felt our bones were stained now indeed and, too shamed to go down to breakfast, we stayed in Joss's room. "But it wasn't our fault," I argued and used a phrase I had read in Monsieur Armand's newspapers, "They drove us to it," but Joss was more truthful than I.

"It was our fault," she said wearily, "and we shall have to learn."

"Learn what?"

"To manage."

"Manage what?"

"Manage what happens to us better than this. I smell," said Joss.

"I smell too," I said.

"Not as badly as I do," and once more she covered her eyes with her hand. It was only to shut out the light but it looked tragic and I felt torn.

When something is badly needed it is amazing how an answer will come. I was moved to tell Joss about Monsieur Joubert. She was quiet as she listened, then she took her hand down. "You mean he said, 'put it on my bill,' just like that?" she asked.

"Just like that."

"He wasn't angry?"

"Not with us."

"And I was drunk."

"Very."

"Like those men by the canal."

"Yes. He carried you up to bed."

"Not . . . Eliot?"

"Eliot wanted to but Monsieur Joubert would not let him."

Joss thought for a moment, then got out of bed, went to the washstand, poured water into the basin, and began to splash her face. She did not speak while she dried her face and hands, then stripped off her crumpled dress; I knew she was thinking very deeply or she would have told me to go away. At last, as she was putting on a clean dress, I asked, "What are you going to do?"

"Give Monsieur Joubert one of my paintings," she said.

"But Joss! He is famous. He gets hundreds of pounds for a portrait. He has paintings in big galleries like the Salon and the Academy."

"Not the Academy. The Uffizi in Florence. They have just bought some of his," said Joss calmly, putting on her shoes.

"He is to have an exhibition in London this year," I argued. "Madame Corbet said so. He—he won't be bothered with a girl, Joss. He is Marc Joubert. Madame Corbet says he is one of the best painters in the world."

"Then he will know when a painting is good," said Joss.

She was, of course, right. Monsieur Joubert did not send her away; he held the little painting at arm's length, looked at it again, put it up on a chair, and went away from it. Nor was he play-acting—I do not think Monsieur Joubert ever acted. We all stood found in a chorus while a familiar catechism began. "You did this yourself?"

"Yes," said Joss, and we nodded.

"No one helped you?"

"No," and we shook our heads.

"Then what are you doing mixing yourself up with other things?" asked Monsieur Joubert.

Joss said uncertainly, "There are other things."

The answer came back, "Not for you."

"I am going to an art school soon," said Joss.

"When?"

"Perhaps when the holidays are over."

"Painters don't have holidays," said Monsieur Joubert. "They don't know how. Why an art school?"

"I need to learn to draw," said Joss meekly.

I thought he would say, "Nonsense," but he nodded. "That won't spoil you. When Madame your mother is better I will speak with her," and he said to me, "Does she talk?"

"Mother?" I asked, startled.

"Mademoiselle." He pointed at Joss.

"Oh! She! Sometimes."

He pounced. "Not all times?"

"Oh no! That's Hester."

"Then," said Monsieur Joubert, "Mademoiselle Joss can come and paint with me. Not near but near enough, but no other child must come," and he said fiercely to the rest of us, "Keep away!"

We nodded again, our eyes wide with respect. This, we knew, was something different from Eliot.

Eliot made one approach to Joss. Before dinner she stayed out on the terrace so that she need not meet him in the bar. Mademoiselle Zizi was talking to some American arrivals and he went out.

"Joss."

"Yes."

"I'm sorry. Joss, I had to do that."

Joss said nothing.

"You won't talk to me?" asked Eliot.

"No," said Joss.

"Tomorrow I'm not going to Paris and—"

"I will be busy tomorrow," and it was true, not an excuse.

From that day we were split as we had been ... before Eliot, I thought. Vicky went back to Monsieur Armand, Willmouse stayed in his cherry-bank atelier, Hester and I rambled alone. Joss got up in the mornings now as early as Monsieur Joubert; almost before it was light she was out on the bank—she too was painting two pictures—and she went early to bed. "There is no light then. I might as well go to bed," she said. The other people in the house hardly saw her at all.

As Hester and I dawdled at the cove we would watch her. She had none of the trappings Monsieur Joubert had, not even a camp stool; she sat on an upturned wooden box and held her board on her knee. She had not any proper canvas, only a piece of linen stretched on the board, but Monsieur Joubert showed her a way of washing it over with two or three coats of white—"not paint, tempera," said Joss—to make it smooth. He had given her a flat tin box filled with jars of tempera and, "One day, he will help me with oils," she said. Worst of all she had no umbrella and she had to sit out in the heat with only her old straw hat to shade her and that had been bent when it was packed so that the straw had split; I could not imagine Joss consenting under any other circumstances to wear it. Every now and then she climbed down the bank and wetted her handkerchief to spread on the crown; even so, she was sickly pale at the end of the day.

"Monsieur Joubert ought to send you in."

"He doesn't notice me," said Joss with pride. She knew how to please him and she only interrupted her work to join us when we went to pay our evening visit to Mother. We were allowed to go and see Mother every day now and, "I'm painting," Joss told her and Mother looked relieved.

"And what are you doing, Cecil?"

"Nothing."

"But you are looking after the Littles?"

"Yes," I said grudgingly. I had to. Joss was as good an elder sister as any but, when she was painting, Vicky or Willmouse could have fallen into the Marne and she would not have known.

"Only they wouldn't," said Hester.

"No, but Willmouse goes off every evening alone and he shouldn't."

Every evening when he had finished his work Willmouse put his things away: his box of scraps, his sewing box, Miss Dawn and Dolores, and their new confections; then he tidied himself, which was only a form because he was always tidy— even his scarecrows managed to be neat; he would wash his face and hands, sleek down his hair with his private bottle of eau de Cologne and, like any old gentleman, go for a little walk. A new barge, the *Marie France 47*, had anchored above the cove; he liked to walk up and look at that.

"Why don't you go when we go?"

"I like to go by myself."

"You can't always do what you like."

"I can," said Willmouse.

I let him. It was too hot, everything was too strained, to bother.

Before Eliot. We were back to that time, yet we were not back. It was the same, and it was not the same. A curious tenseness was in the house. Eliot when he came from Paris looked bone-tired and haggard, and he was so curt with Mademoiselle Zizi that her eyes looked bigger than ever with perpetual tears. She was very silly. She kept searching his face, beseeching him with those big eyes instead of leaving him alone; we scurried out of his way as soon as we saw that tiredness in his face.

For three days he did not come at all. Mademoiselle Zizi went to the telephone four or five times. We heard her ask for the same Paris number, then wait, listening, while that far-off bell rang and rang. There was never any answer. If the office telephone went she would leap out of her chair; then she would sink back again as she heard Madame Corbet's "Hôtel des Oeillets. Oui, Madame. Oui. Certainement."

Then there was Paul. I could bear his having tried to make Joss come to him, that was to be expected of Paul; if he had hit me that night, as I think he meant to with the bottle, I could have expected that too; but he had sneaked out and left me. In our code that was mean.

"Mauricette says you were drunk," said Hester.

"So that was what was the matter with you," said Willmouse.

"She says you shouldn't be with Paul." Hester was troubled.

"He is a horrid boy," said Vicky. "He gave me a bit of frog to eat and said it was chicken."

"Did you eat it?"

"You *can* eat them," said Vicky, as if that settled it.

Neither of the Littles liked Paul. Hester, of course, took a more lenient view. "But you were not there," I said. "You don't know how awful he was," I said.

"More awful than you and Joss?"

"Yes," and then, thinking of what Paul had been through, the camps and the Hôtel-Dieu, the half-Negro sister, I had to say, "I don't know."

I did not want to see all these in Paul but since coming to Les Oeillets I seemed to see a long way into people, even when I did not wish it. "You think of no one but yourselves," Mother had said on that long-ago day on the beach, and how much more comfortable that had been. I seemed to see into everyone and, "There isn't anybody good," I said in misery.

"Yes, there is," said Hester. "Monsieur Joubert."

Perhaps even he was not completely good but he was . . . kept good, I thought; we could see him now, with Joss faithfully behind him, both of them busy. "I wish I had painting or dressage or something," I said and asked, "How can you be good if you are just lying about?"

"Mother says not everyone can have things."

"Then they can't be good," I said firmly.

Hester was looking at the river, at the water eddying down. There was a long silence, then, "Cecil, is Eliot good?" she asked.

The question seemed to fall with a plop into the peaceful water.

"We love him," I said uncertainly. Can one love someone who is not good? That was as much a reversal of our ideas as that the Black Virgin was beautiful.

Is Eliot good? It was a question I would rather not have answered and I was glad when the water-whirls took it away.

CHAPTER XII

It was the third week of August, and the same high summer weather; even in the cove it was hot; hardly a breeze disturbed the willows so that they hung dustily green, not showing their silver; the grass was dusty and untidy, filled with the litter left by Sunday walkers and picnickers; the bulrushes were untidy too; they were ripe and powdering and if we accidentally brushed a spear-rod a stain of brown was left on our skin and clothes. In the orchard the greengages were almost over and at dinner small white grapes appeared on the table. "Are they champagne grapes?" we asked—we had become most conscious of champagne—but Mauricette shook her head. "These are from the Midi. Ours are not ripe till the end of September." And she said, "But you will be here for the vintage, of course."

We did not dispute that. It seemed to us we were here forever. Mother was better but still not out of bed, not even sitting up. Next month the holidays would be over, but there were still three and a half weeks to go and at Les Oeillets each day was like a year. Twenty-three days; twenty-three years. Who bothers what will happen in twenty-three years?

I remember thinking that as. I was lying on my stomach in the sun at the edge of the cove, looking down into the water where hundreds of tiny fish were nibbling at nothing that I could see. If I threw in a crumb they would all dart round it, taking bites, as something sensational would divert us. I supposed a fish's only sensation was food . . . food and death, I thought, watching a big fish hovering over them. Sometimes someone from the town or the hotel would bring a fine net and scoop these little fish up, a hundred or so of them, to fry crisp and season with salt and lemon, and eat with slices of brown bread and butter. I had eaten dozens; now I, part of their fate, hung over them and they did not even see me. Ugh! I thought.

My back seemed to be melting with heat but suddenly I felt cold as if my blood had chilled. There was nothing one could do; at any moment the big fish, the net, might come to any of us, to me. I looked at the nibbling shoal again. If there were a crumb they darted, but even if the shadow of a very big fish went over them they did not move from the crumb. They were too busy living.

Well then, I thought; and slowly the cold ebbed away and again I could feel the heat beating through my dress onto my skin but I could not forget that cold. "Funny, I was never afraid of death before," I told Hester.

"You never thought about it," said Hester and she comforted me. "It was only the fish." I had put death firmly out of my mind when she said thoughtfully, "I don't know why but I don't like these days."

I did not like them either but there seemed nothing wrong, in fact there was a new friendliness in the house. We had put Paul out of bounds so that we heard no scandal; Mademoiselle Zizi and Joss kept truce under Monsieur Joubert; Madame Corbet, perhaps because she wished she had not slapped me, was less sharp; and for us it was as if we had taken a step or two backwards; we were children again, and that was a relief.

Joss finished her first painting and took it to Mother. Vicky had her fifth birthday; Monsieur Armand made her a cake and we had a French birthday party. We were to remember it always. "Because it was from then," said Hester afterwards. "That was the day," she said, "when Eliot began to be where he wasn't."

"And wasn't where he was."

It was a queer birthday party. A table was carried out into the garden, Mauricette covered it with a white cloth and decorated it with vine leaves from the arbour. In the middle was the cake, covered with cream icing and nuts, and round it Mauricette put a ring of wineglasses filled with grenadine. "No tea?" asked Vicky, puzzled, but there was no tea. Mademoiselle Zizi came and Madame Corbet, Mauricette, Monsieur Armand, Toinette and Nicole, Robert the gardener and his wife and baby; Monsieur Joubert and Joss left their painting, Willmouse his sewing. Paul curtly refused to come out of the kitchen, and Eliot, though he had known about the party, had gone to Paris. That made it more amiable but less exciting.

It did not last long; there were no presents, Mother could not be reminded and we could not buy them without any money, but Vicky, with so few birthdays behind her, was not in the habit of presents and did not know what she was missing. We drank her health, cut the cake, and, after eating and drinking, broke up. Joss, Hester, and I went to the hospital, Willmouse took his walk, and Vicky had more cake in the kitchen.

When Willmouse came in he said, "Who told you Eliot was in Paris?"

"He is."

"He isn't. He's here."

"How do you know?"

"I saw him," but Willmouse seemed perplexed.

"What is the matter?" I asked him.

"It was Eliot, not in Eliot's clothes."

"You must have made a mistake."

"I don't make mistakes about clothes," said Willmouse.

He had been walking home along the bank—"You know the bit along the path where the cove is hidden in the bulrushes?"—when Eliot had appeared, walking in front of him. "And he was wearing blue, like the overalls here but trousers and one of those striped jersey shirts."

"Eliot doesn't wear those sort of clothes," said Hester.

"I *know*," said Willmouse, exasperated. "That's why."

"Why?"

"Why it seems funny when he does."

"Are you *sure*?" asked Hester.

"Don't I know about clothes?" said Willmouse in a terrible voice, and Hester subsided.

"He went off the path just above the bulrushes where it has a side path into the wood." Willmouse wrinkled his forehead again. "Do you know it looked—I thought—but he couldn't have . . ."

"Couldn't have what?"

"Come off the new barge." Willmouse sounded oddly positive but what would Eliot have been doing on the *Marie France*?

We liked barges with their black hulls and clean scrubbed decks, and had all been up to look at this one. We often looked into barge cabins to see their shining brass, their curtains and pots of flowers: often there was a cat or a bird in a cage, a mother and lots of children, but the *Marie France* did not seem to have a woman aboard. Her brass was not polished, there were no curtains or flowers. She was a dingy barge and we saw only two men, in the cotton trousers Willmouse had described, but they did not wear jerseys, even cotton ones; they were naked above the waist, with black sailor caps.

"It wasn't Eliot," I said, and that seemed positive when Eliot came back at nine o'clock that night.

"Did you have a good day?" Mademoiselle Zizi asked anxiously.

"Damnably hot," said Eliot. He looked exhausted.

He had brought Vicky a box of chocolates such as we had never seen or imagined; it was a pink satin box painted with roses and tied with wide velvet ribbon and, inside, where most boxes have paper-lace edgings, it had real lace. It was marked "Dorat." "One of the most expensive chocolate shops in Paris," exclaimed Madame Corbet.

"You see he was in Paris," I told Willmouse.

"Yes," said Willmouse, but he did not sound convinced.

Eliot stayed at Les Oeillets next day but he did not sit, as he usually did, reading in the garden. First he took the Littles to see Mother; when he came back he asked Hester and me if we would like to go with him into the town. We passed Joss on the river bank but she did not turn her head nor did Eliot say anything. In the town he bought postcards, giving them to us, and then some grapes for Mother which we took to the hospital, calling on Monsieur le Directeur, who called out, "A ce soir," when we left.

"Why à ce soir?" I asked.

"He is coming tonight. There's a big dinner," said Eliot. "Didn't you know?"

"We are not told things," I said.

As soon as we got in Eliot coaxed Mademoiselle Zizi out to the Giraffe. "That's three times," said Hester.

"That Eliot has gone into the town?"

"Yes. Isn't he fidgety?" said Hester.

He could not have had very much lunch, for just after twelve he came to the cove where Hester and I had taken our picnics and turned us out. "Keep away," he said. "I want to sleep."

"But we haven't eaten our picnics."

"Well, go and eat them somewhere else."

There was no one about. Monsieur Joubert had gone in; he lunched at twelve. Joss could not accompany him; she ate her picnic humbly in the orchard; after that they both went to their rooms to sleep. Willmouse too, after his picnic, would take a nap under his cherry tree; like the little old gentleman he was he would cover his face with his handkerchief. Vicky was still at the age when she was put to rest and was collected by Joss on her own way up. Monsieur Armand, when the luncheons were over, would read the newspaper on the kitchen table, Mauricette lazed in the kitchen or garden, Mademoiselle Zizi lay in a long chair on the terrace, and I think even Madame Corbet nodded in the office. Hester and I had meant to bathe, immersing ourselves, coming out now and again in the sun, going back; the water would have been cool, but now we could not bathe.

Eliot must have divined this for he asked, "Did you want to bathe?" and he suggested, "Go to the Plage for once."

"We should have to pay," said Hester.

Eliot laughed. "You little skinflints."

That hurt us. "Ever since we have been here," I said in a muffled voice, "we haven't had any money."

"Why not?" asked Eliot.

"Nobody has given us any." Hester's voice was muffled too. It was from the remembrance of the times we had looked over at the Plage, read the list of ices, gazed in at the sweetshops in the town, at those wonderfully coloured sucettes and, in L'Eglantine, at the gladioli we had wanted for Mother; it was the remembrance of Vicky not having any birthday presents, of wanting to buy "Moi et Toi" and something for Uncle William that made us sound choked.

"Usually we have pocket money every week," I explained.

"Good lord! I'm sorry," said Eliot. "Why didn't you ask? Look. Have three weeks' now." And he took out his wallet, fat with French notes, and peeled off seven. "One for Hester, one between Vicky and Willmouse, two for Cecil, and three for Joss."

We looked at them, stunned, and neither of us moved. "Take them," said Eliot; he sounded impatient but we shook our heads. "What's the matter now?"

"It's too much," said Hester and I added, "More than a pound each."

"If I say you can have it."

"We can't," said Hester, shocked. "You see, Vicky has six-pence, Willmouse has ninepence, I have a shilling, Cecil has two, and Joss has another arrangement." I would not have told all this, but Hester never minded exposing the family. "She has ten shillings, but she has to pay her bus fares and buy her own stamps and soap and toothpaste and handkerchiefs and stockings."

"Don't. You make me giddy," said Eliot. "Well, have this for now," but we still shook our heads.

"Must you be so appallingly honest?" He said it so harshly that we stared.

"I suppose," said Hester, wavering, "that Mother would pay for us to bathe."

"Look," said Eliot, "I'm tired." He did not seem tired but . . . was it excited? Why? I wondered. Why should he be excited on this hot sleepy afternoon? "Take this." He gave us a note. "Go and bathe and we will settle the rest this evening." We still hesitated and he shouted, "Go! If anyone comes near me before five o'clock I shall skin them alive."

In fairness we ought to have gone and fetched the others when we had finished our picnics but, "They are probably asleep," said Hester. "They can go afterwards. There's heaps of money," and so we went to the Plage we had looked at and yearned after so often. We walked over the white bridge, past the railing with the lifebelt, in at the gate, and took our tickets from the sleepy caretaker; we rented one of the red and white cabins and used all three pools and the low, the middle, but not the high diving boards. I could dive though sometimes I hit the water with a slap. Hester simply jumped off, holding her nose. It was blissfully cool and for an hour or two we were like a pair of porpoises playing. At last we came out and, after we had dressed, we bought strawberry ices from the kiosk and ate them at one of the white tables. "Eliot is good!" said Hester reverently as she licked her cardboard spoon.

The ices were spun out as long as we could. "We had better not have another one, had we?" asked Hester but in the end we had another between us. We spun that one out as well. Four o'clock struck but, "I don't want any goûter," she said; nor did I.

We left the Plage and walked back along the bank; it was then that Hester said, "Let's creep up on Eliot."

"For what?"

"Just to love him," said Hester. Another Eastern idea of which Father had told us was the taking of "darshan," that even to look on anyone good or great would feed the soul.

"He told us not to."

"How will he know?" asked Hester.

Les Oeillets had taught us to be as adept as Red Indians in stealing up on what we wanted to see and we came up to the cove without a sound. Eliot was lying, as he always lay, face downwards on the sand, his length pressed into it, his head pillowed on his arms, the old cap tilted over his eyes. Behind the bulrushes we crept up on him. He was lying with his head towards us. "Fast asleep," breathed Hester.

That must have made a sound, for he stirred, stirred and lifted his head and—it was not Eliot.

In Eliot's clothes, under Eliot's cap, we were looking into the face of a dark unknown man. I do not know why it was so frightening but, for the long moment he looked, we froze as rabbits do and the river seemed to be running in my ears. When his head went down again we retreated backwards through the bulrushes so fast that we were covered in bulrush dust. Then we ran. We reached Joss's box and I sank down on it while Hester fell on the grass. My neck and the backs of my knees were clammy and cold; her chin was shaking.

We sat there a long while without speaking and the sun did not make us any warmer.

At last, "Do you think it could be us—after the ices?" asked Hester.

"No."

"It was another m—"

"Yes."

"Then. . . ?" The question seemed to go on and on.

It was some time later that Hester said, "Hullo! Monsieur Joubert's things have gone." There was no umbrella, no easel or stool, and Joss's box, alone on the river bank, looked small and lonely.

The light grew deeper, swallows were beginning to skim the river as they did when the insects flew down; five o'clock struck from the Hôtel de Ville and we got up to go in. As we reached the blue door it opened and Mademoiselle Zizi came out.

She was in white and carried a deep mauve sunshade, the colour of heliotrope. She was freshly powdered and made up and her scent came to us in waves. "Are you going out?" we asked stupidly.

"Only to the cove, to meet Eliot."

We looked at each other, opened our lips, and shut them.

"Why didn't you tell her?" said Hester after she had gone.

"Why didn't you?"

We did not go in but stayed in the orchard. We talked to Willmouse, admired Miss Dawn's new hat, and played with the dogs. We did not say it to each other but we were waiting to see and, after what seemed a long while, the blue door opened again. Mademoiselle. Zizi came through, and behind her was Eliot.

CHAPTER XIII

As soon as we came into the house we knew that Madame Corbet had sent Mademoiselle Zizi to meet Eliot because she wanted her out of the way.

Madame Corbet was efficient; when anything had to be arranged at Les Oeillets, a dinner, two or three char-à-bancs of tourists for luncheon or an early breakfast, it was made ready quietly and swiftly, "but not if Mademoiselle Zizi is there," said Hester. Mademoiselle Zizi gave contradictory orders to Mauricette, upset Monsieur Armand by suggesting last-minute changes in the food, took Paul away from his work, and quarrelled with Madame Corbet. It was wiser to send Mademoiselle Zizi away and now the house was being quickly transformed; we could see it was for a much bigger occasion than any since we had come.

"Is it a *banquet*?" asked Willmouse.

The tables in the dining room had been moved to make one large T, the whole covered with white cloths and laid with silver and glass, "Ninety-four places," whispered Hester when she had finished counting. The flowers were not being done as usual by Mauricette; Madame from L'Eglantine and her two Mademoiselles in green overalls were arranging them, carnations, asparagus ferns, and white flowers like small lilies on one stem; they had a strong, sweet smell. "Mauricette says they are tuberoses," I said.

"I have heard of them," said Willmouse gravely.

In the bar a platform had been made; we knew it was only of boxes but, laid with a carpet and palms, it looked impressive. There were more flowers in the hall and bar and a carpet had been put down from the front door to the foot of the stairs, "because the Sous Préfet and Monsieur le Maire are coming," said Vicky who had joined us from the kitchen.

We had seen the Mayor of Southstone at the Armistice parade; he had worn a red-caped cloak, a cocked hat, and a great chain. "But I did not know one had mayors to dinner," I said in awe.

"It is a banquet," said Willmouse certainly.

"It's the Brass Instruments Ball," said Vicky, who had been in the kitchen most of the day and knew everything.

Not quite everything. It was the Brass Instrument Factory's centenary dinner, but it remained forever in our minds as the Brass Instruments Ball.

We had often passed the factory when we were exploring across the river and spelled out the lettering on the long notice board along its wall. "Emile Perrichaut, fabricant d'instruments de fanfare. Trompettes. Clairons. Médaille de l'Exposition de 1895. Fournisseur de l'Armée." Now all the thirty workers, with their wives—and husbands, for some of

the workers were women—their grown-up sons and daughters, were coming and, as well as the Sous Préfet and the
Mayor, the Town Clerk, the Commissary of Police, the Lieu-
tenant of Gendarmerie, the Chief of the Municipal Band, "et
le Capitaine des Pompiers," said Mauricette, which meant the
head of the fire brigade. Mauricette said that the doctor, Monsieur le Directeur, was coming because he was the brother-in-
law of Monsieur Perrichaut, and that Eliot and Mademoiselle
Zizi were invited. There would be no room at Les Oeillets for
any visitors that night, the whole hotel was taken up with the
Brass Instruments.

"What will they do?" asked Vicky, and I saw she was trying
to think of the most exciting things she had heard of people
doing. "Drink cider and play cards?" she asked.

"They will eat a lot, drink quite a lot, and make long
speeches," said Eliot, who had come up behind us. Hester and
I shrank a little from him but he did not notice. "And then
perhaps they will dance."

"To the Brass Instruments Band?" asked Hester.

The Brass Instruments had their own band. We had heard
it on Sundays and feast days in the town and guessed that the
platform was for them.

"Look what they are to *eat*!" said Vicky.

She had brought us the menu:

Hors d'œuvres vanés
Homard à la mayonnaise

"That's lobster," I told Vicky.

"I know, I ate some," she said.

Poulet chasseur
Filet de bœuf rôti jardinière
Salade de saison
Fromages variés
Piéce montée
Fruits

"And the pièce has a whole band on top of it," said Vicky. "Monsieur Armand has been four days making it. He said I wasn't to tell you."

She took us to look at it. It was on a silver slab, a great cake with trellises and scrolls of icing and, on top, a sugar band, the bandsmen made of meringue and coloured, the tiny brass instruments of yellow sugar. We could not believe it had been made here in the kitchen. "I am Marc Joubert of the icing sugar," said Monsieur Armand. He seemed radiantly pleased as he chivvied us out of the kitchen but I had caught sight of Paul, his back turned to us, at the sink with a huge pile of saucepans. When he reached for a cloth the lock of hair fell back and we saw his face looking thinner than ever and as dirtily white as his apron. How I wish now I had gone and spoken to him but I was afraid he would only swear at me.

No one told us what was to happen to us and we stayed watching in the dining room while Madame Eglantine and her Mademoiselles put the last flower in the last vase, then we went upstairs and dressed. We put on our best frocks, that we had not worn yet; they were not very grand, crinkled white seersuckers with small rose spots. Mother had made them out of a length she had bought at the sales; Joss had grown out of hers, and they had been handed down so that I wore Joss's,

Hester wore mine and Vicky Hester's; with two more to come down, it seemed Vicky would have to wear rose-spotted seersucker for years. Willmouse put on a clean shirt, his silk tie, clean shorts. "What will Joss wear?" asked Hester.

"She will see when she comes in."

"Isn't she in?" asked Hester, but there was no sound from her room.

We cleaned our nails and brushed our hair; Vicky and Hester put on clean white socks—Joss had arranged for our washing to be done and at last we had clean clothes—I unrolled my one pair of thin stockings, and we cleaned our sandals. When we were finished there still had not been a rustle from Joss's room. "If she had been to see Mother she would have been back long ago. Perhaps she went out with Monsieur Joubert," said Hester.

"Someone would have told us."

I knocked. No answer. I went in and Joss was there, lying face downwards on her bed.

"Joss! Are you having an attack?"

No answer.

I went timidly closer. Hester and the Littles stayed at the door.

"Joss. It's Cecil. Speak to me, Joss."

She raised her head but she did not speak to me. "I hate her. I hate her," she said. It sounded as if she were speaking to the whole world.

"Hate whom?" But I knew and, "What happened?" I asked apprehensively.

"She has ended the painting," said Joss.

"Ended the . . ."

"Yes." Joss sat up and beat the pillow with her fist. "Yes! Yes! Yes!"

"But . . . how?"

"He asked me to have lunch with him."

I hesitated. We knew who "she" was but "he" might have been . . . "Eliot?" I hazarded.

"Idiot! Monsieur Joubert. It was so hot outside—I think he did it because of that—and I said yes. There was no one in the dining room but us and . . . them."

"Mademoiselle Zizi and Eliot?"

"Yes. Madame Corbet was too busy to come in to lunch. Perhaps we—Monsieur Joubert and I—laughed too much." She lifted her chin. "I wanted to laugh . . . Eliot . . ." She broke off.

I had to prompt her. "Eliot?"

"Kept looking," said Joss. "Then, when he had gone—he went quite soon as if he didn't like it—Mademoiselle Zizi came to our table and said . . ." She stopped again.

"Said?"

"It was in French but I understood. I wish I hadn't," said Joss. She looked round and saw the others. "Shut the door, Cecil."

I slowly crossed the little room and shut the door. Whether because of the long bathing that afternoon or the shock in the cove, I seemed to be filled with pains, in my legs and back and head, pains that hurt, and I did not want to hear any more . . . ugliness, I thought—I could sense this was something ugly— and I wished I were with Hester and the Littles on the other side of the door.

I came back to the bed and Joss whispered, "She told him she could not have it in her hotel, an old man and a young girl. That I had . . ."

"Had?"

"Bothered Eliot," said Joss in a whisper. Two tears fell on the pillow, only two; it was as if she were bleeding, not crying.

"What happened then?"

"Monsieur Joubert got up and bowed, not to her but to me."

"*Bowed* to *you?*"

"Yes," said Joss impatiently. "He said, 'When you are a little older and in another place, and your mother is with you, we shall meet again. I shall write to her,' and he left."

"For good?"

"Yes. I saw Paul carry out his luggage and painting things and a taxi came. I don't think Mademoiselle Zizi meant Monsieur Joubert to do that—I heard Madame Corbet being cross—but when she sees me Mademoiselle Zizi can't help what she does. She won't let me have anything. Not anything."

"Why does she hate Joss so terribly?" I asked Hester afterwards. "It seems more than because Eliot likes her."

"It isn't Eliot," said Hester, "not only Eliot," and she added, "You know how, when you have been awful to anyone, you can't bear them."

Now I felt miserably tired, too tired to cope with this hotbed of feelings; it seemed to me the house was filled with them, with hate and love and the love seemed as bad as the hate. Something bad will happen, I thought, and again those prickles of fear ran over me.

"Joss . . ."

I meant to tell her about the man in the cove but she was not listening, at least she was listening to something else. She asked, "What is happening downstairs?"

I told her about the Brass Instruments Ball; the glory had gone out of it for me but she got up from the bed. She looked so determined that I asked, "What are you going to do?"

"Go to the party," said Joss.

"But we haven't been asked."

She did not answer that. She looked over my head and said, "I tried to be nice. I found my own thing and kept out of the way. Now I won't."

"Suppose they don't ask you?"

"I shall make them. I can make people do what I like." By "people" I knew she meant men.

"But Joss"—I produced this hesitantly—"if you make them won't it seem that you might—might be what Mademoiselle Zizi says you are?"

Joss's chin went even higher. "She thinks I am what she is," she said with disdain. "All right. I shall be, only worse." Perhaps she saw the doubt on my face, for she asked, "What else am I to do?"

That sounded like Joss, not Joss cased in this proud hardness, and I said, "Go on painting."

"Without Monsieur Joubert?"

"That's what he would have done."

I thought I had won but when I looked at her I saw it was no use saying anything more. She had on that look again, her mask look, her eyes almost like slits as if she were calculating, her nostrils pinched and her lips set. "I shall go to this party," said Joss, "and I shall wear Sin."

It was called Sin because she had had no right to buy it. A year before Uncle William had given Joss money to buy a new raincoat; her old one was up to her knees and showed inches of wrist, but she had gone into a dress shop and bought a dress. That was in the sales too—"and it had been marked down from ten guineas," said Joss.

"Ten guineas for a dress!" That seemed fabulous to us—except Willmouse.

"A dress can cost a hundred pounds," said Willmouse.

"But . . . when will you wear it?" Mother had asked, bewildered.

"Perhaps never," said Joss, "but I had to have it." It was ivory silk, stamped with roses. "Not many roses," Hester had said critically, "and not much silk." There did not seem much of anything to cost all that money; it left Joss's neck and arms bare and the skirt was narrow. "It's the cut," Willmouse had explained and examined it carefully. "It is influenced by the Chinese," he pronounced, "which is why it suits her."

For a year it had hung in Joss's cupboard. Now, after she had washed her face and brushed her hair, she took it out of the wardrobe. I had opened the door into my room to let the others come and we watched while she put it on.

Beside Sin our seersuckers looked very ordinary and homemade and, in spite of the Black Virgin, the old envy came back. "It's too tight," I said spitefully. "You *show*."

Joss looked at herself in the looking-glass and smiled. "All the better," she said and laughed at my scandalized face. I had noticed while she washed that the dark tufts of hair under her arms were gone. "I have a little razor," said Joss. She had a lipstick and powder too. When she had bought these things I did not know but watched, divided between marvelling and fright while she made up her face. "Don't put on too much," said Willmouse.

"I'm not Mademoiselle Zizi," said. Joss witheringly.

When she was ready her glance fell again on me. "What's the matter with you, Cecil?" she asked.

"I have pains."

"Where?"

"In my arms and legs—everywhere."

"Growing pains," said Joss.

I suppose now it was only an ordinary bourgeois party such as would be held anywhere in the provinces of France, but to us it seemed resplendent and exciting, though we had to admit the guests were not as elegant as the flowers and food. "I think I shall go for my evening walk," said Willmouse after we had seen the first few people arrive. I could tell he was disappointed. We had not taken it into account that they were working people not quite at home in their Sunday best. The men were in dark suits, too heavy for the hot evening, and they wore thick-soled shoes; they all seemed to show a great deal of gold watch chain and cuff links. Their wives had meticulously clean blouses, coats and skirts, and wore high-heeled shoes instead of their usual slippers.

We watched from the stairs, not daring to risk going down until there were so many people that Mademoiselle Zizi or Madame Corbet would not notice us.

"Is that Monsieur le Maire?" asked Hester. Everyone bowed politely as they greeted him, but though his beard was imposing he was wearing a plain black suit and had only a little ribbon in his buttonhole to show he was important, no scarlet cloak, cocked hat, or chain. The Sous Préfet, more important than he, had not even a ribbon but Monsieur Perrichaut was impressive; we knew it must be Monsieur Perrichaut because he was receiving with his wife. He was taller than anyone else— "Except Eliot," said Hester—white-haired, with an important-looking paunch. "Let me look at him," said Joss and gazed as if she were spying out the land. Monsieur Perrichaut seemed fitted to be the owner of the Brass Instruments Factory; his voice was like a saxophone and when he blew his nose the noise was like a trumpet. He had a young man at his elbow who made introductions in a reedy voice. "Like a piccolo," I whispered but Joss did not laugh. She was very grave. "Tell me when the doctor comes."

"Monsieur le Directeur?"

"Yes."

"He is here," said Vicky presently.

"Go down," Joss told us. "Go one by one, slip in among them and start shaking hands with everyone. Then they can't send you away. And don't tag on to me," she said severely.

Hester and Vicky disappeared but I hung back. Joss hummed a little tune—which told me she was nervous— twitched the skirt of her dress straight, frowned at it, shook her hair more loosely on her shoulders, and went down. I watched her as she went straight to the doctor, holding out her hand; then I followed, keeping behind the crowd.

The doctor kept Joss's hand. "Mais . . . c'est la petite Anglaise!" he said. I edged round to see her better.

She was making a comical face—a moue, I thought wisely. "Not so little," she said, and appealed to Monsieur Perrichaut, "I am not very little, pas si petite, am I, Monsieur?" Hester had crept up beside me. "She sounds silly—like a lady," said Hester disapprovingly.

Silly or no, Monsieur Perrichaut seemed to like it. Soon he was asking her, "Vous dînez avec nous, Mademoiselle?"

"He *is* asking her to dinner," I told Hester.

"I—I have not been invited," said Joss. She sounded as if she were pretending to be shy and Hester and I both frowned.

"Je vous invite," and the piccolo was sent to tell Madame Corbet to set another place. "A côté de moi," said the doctor gallantly.

"Monsieur le Directeur s'y connaît," said Monsieur Perrichaut. The most important people were standing round him and now Joss was in the centre of them. Everyone was whispering about her. Mademoiselle Zizi had seen her but she could not very well send her out.

"Permettez-moi de vous faire mes compliments, Mademoiselle." That was the Sous Préfet.

"Ah! La jeunesse! La jeunesse!" said Monsieur Perrichaut and they gazed at Joss.

"Absolument ravissante," said Monsieur le Maire. He was standing just in front of me and began to discuss Joss's looks with the man beside him; I could not catch it all but I heard, "Ce teint lumineux!"

"What are they saying?" hissed Hester.

"Compliments," I hissed back.

Eliot was by the bar talking to the young Town Clerk, whom Mauricette pointed out to me because she admired him. The Town Clerk was dark and good-looking, but Eliot could look over his head and the heads of most of the others. Joss must have seen him at once but she appeared not to see him nor did he look at her. I did not like this any more than I liked her pretending to be shy. Things had gone . . . out of truthfulness, I

thought. Before we had been unhappy but it was truthful, now
we seemed to be playing a game, and I walked away from them
all out onto the terrace where it was cool and quiet. Presently
it would be moonlight, a scented, moonlit summer night, but
that seemed to me to make this playing worse, expose it more.
I put my elbows on the warm iron rail and leaned my head on
my hands, hiding my eyes as if I did not want to see, to look or
think, but I was not left in peace for long. Fairy lights had been
strung between the trees and now they came on, red and blue
and yellow. "Ah! C'est joli!" cried a woman and people came out
onto the terrace to see. Eliot was with them and it was then that
the next odd thing happened.

I heard my name called; Willmouse was running across
the garden. He did not usually run but now gravel spurted up
behind him, his socks were falling down, *Willmouse's* socks. I
ran down the steps to meet him. "Cecil, a most e'straordinary
thing."

As soon as he reached me he began to tell it though he was
half out of breath. "I was having my walk along the river when
I saw a man . . ."

I stiffened. "A . . . dark man?"

"Like Madame Corbet," said Willmouse and I knew he
meant swarthily dark . . . as ours had been, I thought. "He
came out of the bushes," said Willmouse, "and he had a motor
bike; it was a big new red one, at least it looked new. He
wheeled it along the bank and then onto the plank bridge to
the barge . . ."

His voice, shrill with wonder and speaking English, must
have carried to the terrace. I saw Eliot come to the rail and
look down.

"Onto the *Marie France*?" I asked Willmouse.

"Yes. The man looked up and down the river as if he wanted to see if anyone was there. He couldn't see me—"

"Why not?"

"Because the bulrushes are so tall. Then do you know what he did?" Willmouse paused. He was always dramatic. "He-wheeled-the-bike-across-the-deck-and dropped-it-over-the-other-side," said Willmouse.

"Into the *river*?"

"Yes."

"Don't be silly."

"He did. Cecil, it was a new—"

"And what are you doing out so late?"

Eliot's voice cut across me and it was the voice he had used that first morning when he came out of Mademoiselle Zizi's room; I had heard it again in the courtyard at Dormans. He had left the terrace and come down the steps. "Where have you been?" he said to Willmouse.

"F-for my walk." Willmouse was so startled that the words would hardly come.

"Willmouse always goes for a walk," I said defensively.

"You be quiet," said Eliot and to Willmouse, "You know quite well you are not allowed out so late." Willmouse opened his lips again but, "Not a word," said Eliot. "I will not have disobedience. You can go to bed at once," and he wheeled Willmouse round, a hand on his shoulder.

"But *Eliot*! You *never* . . ." I think I wailed it. It was terrible to see Eliot taking Willmouse up the steps and marching him away like a prisoner. As for Willmouse, he looked grey with shock.

"Mais, Monsieur Eliot"—that was one of a group of men—
"vous êtes trop dur."

"In England we discipline boys," said Eliot crisply; to Willmouse he said loudly, "How often have I told you . . ." And at
once I knew that Eliot was acting.

Acting on Willmouse! I pushed my way after them
to the foot of the stairs. "You have never told him," I cried
passionately.

"Cecil, stay where you are," said Eliot. His face made
me quail but I only stayed there until he came down, then,
challenging him with a look that I hoped was hate, I walked
straight up, but the door of our room was locked. I went into
Joss's room and tried the door there; it was locked as well. I
rattled the handle. "Willmouse, it's Cecil. It's Cecil." There was
no answer. I was not surprised. Willmouse was always still
and silent if he was offended.

I went back to the landing, where I had another pain and
with it such a sense of desolation that I could hardly bear it.
If this was growing—Joss had said that was what the pains
were—I did not like it. Down below the party must have been
going in to dinner; I heard chairs scraped back, more bursts
of laughter, voices. I wondered if Joss was sitting next to the
doctor, if Hester and Vicky were there.

There is nothing more melancholy than listening to a party
from which one is shut out. I could hear the noise of knives
and forks now with the talk and laughter, while on the landing
it was growing dark; the stairs were lit only by the light coming up from the hall; smells of food drifted up with the scent
of flowers and I thought of Willmouse's banquet and gave
a little sob. He was locked in by this inexplicable Eliot and

only I cared, mounting guard beside him, but a guard with a bad pain and half in tears. "Willmouse. Willmouse." Still no answer. I could imagine him rigid with shock. "I *hate* Eliot," I said. Then I jumped. In his cat-quiet way he had come up the stairs and was laughing at me.

When he saw the tears he stopped laughing. He said, "I'm sorry. I had to do that."

"Willmouse is *little*. He wanted to see a banquet."

He said, "I know," and then, "I am not as bad as you think." He was carrying a tray; on it was the chicken chasseur from the menu keeping warm under a small glass cloche, gaufrette potatoes, some of what we called "party toast," toast melba, butter, a meringue and glass of grenadine; it was a bit of the banquet but I was not going to relent.

"He won't eat it," I said distantly.

"We shall see," said Eliot. He unlocked the door but kept me out. "Leave him to me," he said.

I went into the Hole because something had happened to my pain; there, in that smelly little cup: board, I found out.

Even there wonder overcame me. Wonder and fear. I shivered. ". . . with reluctant feet/Where the brook and river meet," Mr. Stillbotham had said; no matter how reluctant, one was pushed into the full tide. Dazed, I came out of the Hole and went into Joss's room and found what I needed in her drawer. It was no use trying to reach her, she was at dinner . . . and so is Mademoiselle Zizi, I thought. Madame Corbet, Mauricette were busy. I had to manage for myself with those strange first necessities of being a woman, and it was inexpressibly lonely. When I was comfortable I began to cry with excitement and self-pity. I was still crying when I went back on the landing.

I could hear Eliot's voice inside our room; then I thought I heard Willmouse give a tiny laugh like a crow. Eliot was even more of a magician than I thought. Always if Willmouse was punished he did not speak for at least two days. I listened and, yes, I heard him laugh again. Then Eliot came out. "Still here?"

"Yes," I said, muffled.

"I think he will eat it all," said Eliot. "He liked the drink."

"You needn't lock the door!" That came out like a cry.

"I said I would and I must," said Eliot. "I will come up later." Then he looked at me. "You are in a state, Cecil. What is the matter?"

He should not have asked that; the tears came flooding.

"Is it Willmouse still?"

I shook my head.

"What is it then?" He put his arm round me, bending down. "Tell?"

Who could resist Eliot when he was Eliot? Eliot, not that other cold stranger. "Never talk to anyone about these times," Mother had said when she told us, "especially not to a man. Women should be private." In Southstone I think I should have shrunk suitably from telling Eliot but Les Oeillets was different and it came out with a rush. "I . . . have turned into a woman."

I did not know how else to put it—Mother had not taught us any of the words—but Eliot did not laugh. He asked, "Just now?"

"Just now," and the tears flowed.

"That isn't anything to cry about," said Eliot gently.

"It . . . hurts."

"Not when you consider how exciting it is."

"Exciting?" That was unexpected.

"Of course."

"But . . . how?"

"Because now you are ready for love."

Love! Probably nothing in the world that Eliot could have said at that moment could have helped me more. Love! Like Mademoiselle Zizi, Juliet, Cleopatra, Eve, like . . . Joss, level with Joss. "I, Cecil," I whispered, dazzled.

"You."

"But . . ." The tears came back. "I am not pretty like Joss."

"You are not pretty like Joss. You are pretty like Cecil."

With my Bullock sturdiness, my pinkness and mouse hair? "I, pretty?"

"Very," said Eliot, and he kissed me on the mouth.

"That scoundrel," Uncle William called him. I only know that night he seemed like an angel to me.

He had to go to dinner but he took me downstairs and put me to sit in the office, which was empty; somehow, in the rush and hubbub, he got Toinette, who was motherly, to make me some tea. How did he know there were only two things in the world I could have swallowed, things English and familiar, bread and butter and tea? I had not known tea could be had in France, though it was tea such as we had not seen, served in a glass, the leaves in a little paper bag tied with a string and soaking in hot water. It was weak but it was hot and I made it sweet and ate four slices of bread and butter. The pain had the edge taken off it now and Toinette patted me and called me "pauvre gosse." Soon I felt much better.

It was a long peaceful wait until people began to come from dinner to dance or sit at the tables in the bar. I stole out on the stairs to watch. Nobody noticed me and I was glad. Then Hester came to sit beside me; she had been dancing and was excited. "Joss is the belle of the ball, isn't she?" she said.

Everyone wanted to dance with Joss. When the men tapped one another on the shoulder, taking one another's partners, she changed partners all the time; she was flushed, far more excited than Hester, but that game was going on. Eliot danced with Mademoiselle Zizi, with some of the wives and daughters, with Vicky and Mauricette, but he never seemed to see Joss nor Joss him; she carefully looked away when they passed; she smiled at her partner and tossed her hair back and fluttered her lashes up and down. "Is that flirting?" asked Hester, but I was beginning to see there was another kind of growing pain. I knew Joss was miserable and I ached for her.

"Qui a laissé ces trucs-là dans mon bureau?" Madame Corbet had found the tray with my plate and tea glass. "Is the whole house to be a nursery?" she scolded and I had to take them to the kitchen. On the way back I had to wait at the service door. They were dancing the carpet dance, the dance du tapis, when the men make a circle and a woman takes a little square of carpet and stands in the centre. When the music stops she kneels down on the carpet in front of the man she chooses, who kisses her and dances with her while everybody claps. He takes her into the circle and this goes on till all the women are in it. The crowd had moved back against the wall to watch the dance and I could not get past. As I stood, there was a loud sound of eating in my ear, a smell of sweat and garlic, Paul; and I had another glimpse of what it was like to be Paul. His face and neck were glistening with sweat, his hair hung limply, his apron and shirt were soaked and covered with stains. He must have been washing up for hours and had taken a moment to eat; he had a piece of sausage clamped in a length of split bread, as he used to make our goûter.

We shouldn't have sent him to Coventry, I thought, and this time was going to make myself speak to him when I saw he had not noticed me; he was watching Joss. When people are watching they forget to pretend and there was something in Paul's face that made me afraid; it was wild, like a wild animal that does not think of itself or any other animal but only of what it wants. Then I learned part of the explanation of why he looked like that; Monsieur Armand called impatiently and Paul turned to go but left the door open and I saw him take a bottle from the shelf behind the door; he tilted it right up before he drank so that I knew it was almost empty. When he put it back he nearly missed the shelf and a moment after I heard a crash of plates.

He came back. Three or four times I noticed him in that door and then I saw that Joss was smiling at him. She only smiled because she was smiling at everyone but, "It *is* flirting," Hester said disapprovingly when I got back to the stairs.

It grew late. Some of the people were going home. Vicky had fallen asleep on a sofa; Madame Corbet looked at her two or three times, then picked her up and carried her to bed. The Brass Instruments Band had finished but a pianist and violinist had taken its place. The music sounded very quiet after the band and the notes of the violin came softly across the floor, sweet with a faint throbbing that made it sound tender.

Joss was standing just below us and for the moment she was without a partner. I think she hoped she would be left without one, for she turned this way and that and I was sure she was looking for Eliot. Then she saw him and for the first time that night they looked at each other. She stood still and I knew her eyes would not plead, only look, unmistakably look. She had had to humble herself to do that, but Eliot walked away to the bar. I clenched my fists. Was Eliot quite impervious? To the throbbing music that seemed to us so beautiful? To Joss? Eliot, who had kissed me upstairs? It was only a moment; the next, Joss was smiling at the piccolo, at the Town Clerk; then she smiled and waved at someone else. I looked to see and it was Paul. The wave was too much. He gave a tug at his apron that broke its string, wrenched it from his neck and threw it away, combed his hair with his fingers, and reached her before the piccolo, who was weaving through the dancers. "Mademoiselle Joss," said Paul and bowed.

If he had been clean it might have been different. Mauricette had danced, and Monsieur Armand, "but not Toinette or Nicole," said Hester. Monsieur Perrichaut called out sharply and a gentleman, who Mauricette told us was Monsieur Rufour of the Commissariat, came up and said to Paul as he stood just below us, "Et toi, mon gaillard, rentre chez toi et restes-y." Monsieur Dufour was, I suppose, in charge of Paul, but Paul had emptied all of that bottle and he shouted so that the words were heard through all the rooms above the music, "Galeux! Gros dégueulasse!" to Monsieur Dufour.

Other men came up; the older ones talked soothingly but the Town Clerk took hold of Paul, who shook him off.

"Paul! Fais-pas l'imbécile," cried Mauricette and ran for Madame Corbet.

"Rentre," said Monsieur Dufour curtly, "C'est ce que tu as de mieux à faire," but Paul had Joss by the hand.

Joss did not know what to do. Gently she tried to take her hand away. "Dance me," said Paul in his poor English.

"They don't want me to," said Joss.

"Foutez-nous la paix!" Paul shouted at them. "Elle n'est pas une sacrée snob."

Without his apron Paul looked tall and, in his untidiness and dirt, almost savage among those Sunday clothes. Joss shrank from him though she was trying not to shrink. "Attendez, Paul," she said. "Wait," but he was putting his arm round her when suddenly between them was Eliot.

He had cut in front of Paul so quickly that no one had seen him come up and almost from inside Paul's arm he took Joss and danced with her away down the room. At the same moment Monsieur Dufour caught Paul by the shoulder, the Town Clerk took his other side, and between them they marched him to the door where Madame Corbet and Monsieur Armand were waiting. "Tordu!" shouted Paul as they took him away. "Pelé! Galeux! Fumier!" The words died away along the passage. Hester was crying, "Poor Paul! Poor Paul!" I felt too miserable to speak.

Joss and Eliot did not speak either as they danced. She kept her eyelids down so that her face looked closed; Eliot's was set.

The music stopped when they were by Mademoiselle Zizi, who had come to the foot of the stairs and was watching. Eliot slowly took his arm away but kept Joss's hand. Joss's chin began to shake. For a moment I thought they would make it up, that he would take her into the garden in the moonlight among the fairy lights, but Eliot did another of his incomprehensible things—"He was trying to look after her," said Hester, "he always did look after us"—he held out his free hand to

Mademoiselle Zizi, who gave him her hand wonderingly. He put Joss's into it. "Take her to bed, Zizi," he said.

"No!" They said it together. Joss's was a curt refusal, while Mademoiselle Zizi sounded as if she were being stifled. "No!"

"Yes," said Eliot gently and inexorably. "The party is over now." He turned away abruptly and said, "Good night."

"Eliot, where are you going?" It was a cry from Mademoiselle Zizi.

"Into the garden to smoke," he said, still gently, and stepped outside.

CHAPTER XIV

Cecil. Cecil."

I had been asleep . . . one minute, I thought, and Joss was standing by my bed. She had put her cold hand under the bedclothes and was clutching me. "Cecil."

My eyelids seemed to have weights of sleep on them. I could not open them.

"Cecil."

"Wh-what is it?"

"Ssh! Don't wake Willmouse."

"What is it?" but I had sunk my voice lower, jerked awake now by her cold and shivering.

"It's Paul."

"Paul?"

"On a ladder, looking in at my window."

"*Paul* is?"

"Yes. He is coming in."

"What for?" I said stupidly but Joss only shivered and said, "Oh Cecil!"

Then I knew it was true and fear started up as I remembered that look on his face at the dance, but some wisdom saved me from telling Joss. "He has been drinking," was all that I said.

"What can we do?" she asked. Her teeth were chattering.

There was only one thing to do and I sat up. "I will get Eliot."

"No!" She sounded outraged.

"But—"

"Don't you *dare*!"

"Then. . . ?"

Joss reluctantly said, "I will go and call Madame Corbet."

"You can't do that."

"Why?"

"She will send Paul away." We were whispering like conspirators. "He will lose his summer bonus and not get his lorry."

"I don't care about his lorry. I must get Madame Corbet or he will come in." She was shaking and I made up my mind. I know now it was of those moments when one is more noble than one is capable of being. I turned back the bedclothes. "Get in," I said. "I will go and talk to Paul."

"But . . ."

"I'm not afraid of Paul," but as I said it, that was not true; I was afraid of that look in him, of the words he had shouted as he was taken away, but Joss was horridly easy to convince—it seems to me now she was astoundingly selfish; she agreed at once. "You are sure you don't mind? It isn't you he has come for," she said, "so you will be all right."

Slowly, fearfully, I opened the door but Paul was not in Joss's room. There was no sign of him and I slid along the wall and into her bed with a feeling half of relief and half of flatness. Then, with a thrill of fear, I saw that, though no one was there, the two ends of the ladder were against the sill.

I knew then a little of what it must have been to be a Grecian maiden, Polyxena, for instance, bound on the faggots or, perhaps not as noble as that, one of the goats Father had told us about, tied up as bait for a tiger. Paul was a little like a tiger and tigers have no pity. What would he do when he found I was not Joss? Would he do what he wanted to do to her? Besides being frightened I was filled with a dreadful curiosity. I had Eve's Curse, that meant I could have a baby although my breasts were only like lemons; they were tingling and I remembered Paul's hand on them and my thighs tingled too.

Faint and far, I heard the Hôtel de Ville clock strike three times. I remembered that afterwards, three o'clock, and then I heard the ladder creak as somebody came up. I gripped the clothes round me and lay as flat as I could in the bed, my heart beating so that I could hardly breathe but, oddly, in the top of my head. My cheeks were hot, and my eyes stretched to see what they must see. It was not Paul coming up the ladder, it was an animal thing, the tiger. A head and shoulders rose black outside the window, dark with a white patch of face—I had almost expected to see it striped—a hand shook the catch loose so that it fell, the window slowly opened.

I screamed, though without a sound. Nothing hurts as much as a scream in silence. Eliot! Eliot! Eliot! It was a scream, a wild prayer; and I heard footsteps running on the gravel.

The ladder and its figure lifted backwards into the air. Paul gave a cry, half muffled, an animal's cry, as he disappeared and there was a thud. The ladder had fallen backwards onto the courtyard grass.

I slid out of bed and crept to the window to look. I remember I was so clammy with fear that the night air struck icily on me and I shivered as Joss had as I looked down.

The ladder lay on the grass; it must have spun as it fell and fallen hard, for it was still quivering, but Paul was standing up, miraculously jumped clear or fallen off. He was standing, though rubbing his elbow and knees, and facing him was Eliot.

Then Eliot had come; but how? How had he heard me? His room was not on this side, nobody's was except Joss's and the visitors' rooms on the first floor which were empty now. Then my sense woke up. How could Eliot have heard me when I had not made a sound? And what was he doing in the garden in the middle of the night—or not the middle, three o'clock in the morning?

Paul was still without his apron and again I saw that without the long white limp garment he looked a man; all at once it seemed possible, even fitting, that he should drive a lorry. It was no longer like Willmouse's atelier, half a child's dream. Eliot was not as usual, either; he-was wearing... and I stopped.

Was he Eliot? What made me so sure he was? This man was in what Willmouse had said Eliot once wore, "not Eliot's clothes," cotton trousers, a striped jersey, the cap. The sight of the cap brought back the fear when that face had looked at us, the dark man's face. In the moonlight I strained to see who it was and yes, it was Eliot. Yet that made me more afraid. I saw the glint of his eyes as he lifted his head and . . . what was he *doing*? As I asked that I saw what I had not noticed before, a small case on the grass. He must have dropped it when he ran to the ladder. Then was Eliot going away? The case was too small to count as luggage but suddenly I knew Eliot was going away.

I think Paul knew that too. I thought I heard him say, "Vous partez, hein?" with some swear words, though it was too far for me to catch the whole of the quick French.

"Ssst!" That came from Eliot like a whipcrack, a warning, but Paul was drunk, drunk and angry, I thought, and . . . "balked" was the animal-sounding word that came into my mind, as he had been balked from dancing with Joss. Now he was daring to bait Eliot. "Vous partez, hein?"

He went nearer. Out of my small experience I could have told him not to go near Eliot when Eliot was that cold stranger, but Paul made a sudden sideways lunge at the case.

I could not see what happened then, who hit whom. Paul's arms went as they had done when he battered me, but Eliot was fighting as . . . one must not fight, I thought appalled. "Never hit in the stomach or kick," Uncle William had taught us, but I saw Eliot's knee come up into Paul and Paul let out a sound as if he were torn; then he doubled over, took two or three steps bent across the grass, made a noise like a gurgle, and fell on his knees and was sick, his hands beating at his chest, his head wagging.

Eliot waited. I can see him waiting now, nothing seemed as cruel as that, and then he was . . . unfair again, but it was worse than unfair, it was cowardly and—a word from school plays came back to me—dastardly. "Never hit anyone who is down," that was Uncle William too but, as Paul's head bent lower, Eliot struck down at his back. It was so quick I could hardly believe I saw it, like lightning. What made it truly like lightning was that, in the moonlight, I thought I saw a long thin thing flash in Eliot's hand. For an odd moment I thought it was his paper knife . . . but he would not carry a paper knife in the garden.

Paul slid gently forwards onto the grass, face downward. His legs kicked once or twice, then there were only quivers, like the ladder.

Eliot looked towards the house, along the windows. I shrank behind the curtains. I could not bring myself to look at his face below the cap; I think I expected it to change into that other man, the third Eliot. There was our Eliot and the cold unkind one, and him. When I looked again he had lifted Paul; he stood a moment, put Paul down, and moved the case, putting it under the bushes. Then he came back to Paul, lifted him again, and carried him away round the house.

What had I seen? I did not know. I remember only that heart beating in the top of my head and I seemed to have turned to ice against the window. I could not even shiver. I looked out into the garden where there was nothing but the garden and the moonlight, a few marks on the grass, and the ladder. I could not believe there had been anything else, been that . . . But what was that? What had Eliot done to Paul? As I asked the question I seemed to hear Eliot's voice saying, "I'm sorry. I had to do that." Then. . . ? Then. . . ?

I do not know how long I stood there by the curtain, my hands on the sill. It might have been a few minutes, it might have been half an hour, but suddenly as I looked down I saw Eliot was back.

He was alone. I do not know why that frightened me but I could not bear it that he was alone.

He came to the ladder, at which he looked down consideringly. It had left marks in the grass, two long scars. I thought he was wondering if he should take the ladder away when, through the night, came a sound that might have been a low hoot from the river or an owl. Eliot turned and picked up the small case.

Once again he scanned the house and again I shrank back against the curtain. Then he was gone.

When I took my hands from the sill the marks of them were there, soaking wet.

CHAPTER XV

It was a morning filled with absences. That sounds contradictory, but it was the absences that made themselves felt. There were two char-à-banc parties for breakfast, Americans on their way from Germany to Paris, and we saw once again how hard hotel people worked. Mauricette told us that when the Brass Instruments Ball had finished it had been past one o'clock but she, Madame Corbet, and Paul had had to set to work, sweep out the dining room and hall, and lay sixty places for breakfast. "And they will not have coffee and rolls," Vicky told us: "They will have grapefruit, bacon and eggs, hot rolls, jam, coffee and tea and milk." Monsieur Armand, Madame Corbet, and Mauricette had to get up at half past six; we knew that because we were waked by cries for Paul.

A long time had gone by last night before I had taken myself out of that room and got into my own bed with Joss and Willmouse. All I could think of was how heavenly warm she was.

"Well?" She had been wide awake.

Why did I not tell her what I had seen? "I have seen nothing, nothing at all," that was what I was saying over and over
again in my head, and aloud I said briefly, "He has gone."

"Are you sure?"

"Quite sure."

I had imagined myself lying awake, seeing it over and over
again, but at once I had fallen asleep.

"Paul. Pa-ul. *Paul!*" That was Mauricette. Then came
Madame Corbet's steps and she flung open our door, "without
knocking," as Joss observed. Madame Corbet was too hurried
to see we were three in the bed together and she did not scold
us. "Have any of you children seen Paul—Paul Brendel?" She
always spoke as if we did not know him.

It was a relief to see Madame Corbet. If she wanted Paul
I could not believe he would not come. "When did you see
him?" she asked.

"At the party last night," said Joss.

"Tscha!" And Madame Corbet shut the door.

Wakened by the noise, Hester and Vicky came in. We were
all awake now, in spite of our late night, wide awake, except
Willmouse, who was fast asleep on the far side of our bed. Nor
would he wake.

"Madame Corbet, Willmouse, our little brother, hasn't
woken."

"Then wake him."

"We—we can't."

Everyone was out of temper that morning and Madame
Corbet snapped, "What is wrong with him?"

Nothing was wrong with him except that he was asleep,
fast asleep, pale, but he was often pale. When we shook him

his head rolled, when we opened his eyelids his eyes showed the whites. "I don't like that," said Hester. It certainly looked alarming. We sat him up but he sagged back on the pillow. He was cold and breathing a little strangely. "Is he ill or asleep?" I asked.

"I don't think you sleep when you are ill," said. Joss. "He is just . . . too asleep."

That was what we told Madame Corbet. "Grands Dieux!" she said. "Why worry me for that? Let him sleep."

When ten o'clock came and he had not stirred we began to worry more. The house was swarming with the Americans; they were taking snapshots of the staircase, of the place under the urn where Rita and Rex had found the skull—as it was so early and Paul had not been found, the bloodstain was left out—and there was no hope of getting anyone to look at Will-mouse. Joss made up her mind. "I'm going to the hospital," she said.

"To tell Mother?" I spoke out of my yearning; inexpress-ibly that morning I was longing for Mother.

"Don't be an idiot," said Joss, "I am going to ask Monsieur le Directeur if Willmouse is all right."

"You could telephone."

"I can't in French. I don't know how to get the number," and Hester said, "I *wish* Eliot were here."

Eliot's was the third absence. He had gone to Paris, Made-moiselle Zizi told the Monsieur from the Police, Monsieur Dufour, who came asking questions.

I had come into the hall on my way upstairs; the char-à bancs had driven away, Les Oeillets was quiet again, but in the hall was Monsieur Dufour sitting on a chair, rubbing his chin with the end of his cane, his hat on one of the console tables. I was examining him out of the corner of my eye when Mademoiselle Zizi came from her room. She was in a pale green dressing-gown, her hair twisted up, her face just as it was without rouge; she suddenly looked to me most beautiful.

"I regret I kept you waiting, Monsieur."

"Une demi-heure," said Monsieur Dufour but he did not sound angry. His eyes were brown and very kind. He kept them on Mademoiselle Zizi.

They spoke in French but I could follow them. "I wanted to see Monsieur Eliot," said Monsieur Dufour, "but Irène says he is not here."

"He has gone to Paris, Monsieur."

"At three o'clock in the morning." I wondered what effect it would have on them if I had said that.

"He has a business there?"

"So I understand."

I began to think there was some deep feeling between these two; Monsieur was warmer to Mademoiselle Zizi than she to him; she still distantly called him "Monsieur."

"How did he go to Paris if his car is here?"

Now I came to think of it the Rolls was on the drive outside. It had not been there last night, but Mademoiselle Zizi was explaining. "Since yesterday Fouret's have had it for graissage. Today Monsieur Eliot drove up with friends. Look, Fouret's tag is on the windscreen if you wish to see it, Monsieur."

She minds his questions about Eliot, I thought, and he does not like asking them. It makes him feel awkward. "This is a routine check on all strangers in the town, Zizi," he said. "We have nothing against Monsieur Eliot."

"What could you have?" asked Mademoiselle Zizi, more cold then ever, but he went quietly on with his questions.

"He stays here?"

"Is that a fault?"

"Zizi. I *have* to ask. Please understand."

"You know he stays here. The whole town knows."

"Yes," said Monsieur Dufour. He sounded sorrowful but he went on. "He was here at the dinner yesterday evening?"

"You saw him," said Mademoiselle Zizi.

"But he went to Paris in the day?"

"No."

"No?" asked Monsieur Dufour.

"He was here all day." And she flashed, "He was here in the bar writing letters. Then he took an early lunch and spent the afternoon in the cove." Her eye fell on me trying to make myself small. "If you do not believe me, ask this child," said Mademoiselle Zizi.

My stomach gave a sudden unexpected heave. I thought I was going to be sick. Monsieur Dufour turned those kind brown eyes on me. "Did you see Monsieur Eliot in the cove?"

"Yes, Monsieur."

His eyes dwelt on me a moment . . . did he guess there was something else? Then I felt a soft little touch on my elbow; it was Hester, as usual. Monsieur Dufour passed to her.

"And did you see Monsieur Eliot in the cove?"

"Yes, Monsieur." It came out patly. I do not know how we agreed silently not to tell. Hester added, "He gave us money to go bathing."

"You see!" cried Mademoiselle Zizi, then she burst out indignantly, "But why should you ask questions? You *know* Eliot."

"I know him," said Monsieur Dufour, and again he sounded sad, "but I have to make my report."

He had picked up his hat when Madame Corbet came out of the office. "Have you said anything about Paul?" she asked Mademoiselle Zizi.

"Paul. Ah yes!" And Mademoiselle Zizi turned to Monsieur Dufour again. "I suppose it is you we have to tell. It is Paul Brendel, the boy you sent me."

"He was troublesome last night. What now?"

"Only that he seems to have gone," said Madame Corbet.

The strange morning went on. I remember I was cold, though it was the same brilliant heat, so that even Madame Corbet, sitting in the office, had beads of sweat caught in her moustache and patches of wet on her blouse. As the day went on the coldness seemed confirmed, inexorably, as if hope were slowly frozen out.

The doctor came to see Willmouse. Madame Corbet brought him upstairs. "Sixty people to breakfast, the dinner last night, and now they imagine illness," she said. "These children think they own the whole hotel."

She stood at the bedroom door while Monsieur le Directeur bent over Willmouse and listened to his breathing; he felt his pulse and then raised one of Willmouse's eyelids and looked into his eye that still looked horrible with its rolled-up white. "He is tired out with excitement," said Madame Corbet, "so he sleeps."

"Il a été drogué," said Monsieur le Directeur.

"Drogué? What is drogué?" asked Joss.

It was Madame Corbet who answered in a bewildered voice, "Drugged."

"*Willmouse?*"

Monsieur le Directeur was asking if there were any sleeping tablets in the house that Willmouse could have found. "Coloured ones like sweets," he suggested in French. "Yours?" he asked Madame Corbet. "No, you would not leave them about. Zizi's?"

"I keep Zizi's," said Madame Corbet. She added that it was impossible.

Impossible, but it had happened. Standing at the foot of the bed with Joss, I knew it was not impossible. Unwillingly I knew more. While they had been talking I had seen that supper tray again and the grenadine and heard Eliot's voice saying smoothly, "He liked the drink." But why? I thought giddily, why? Then I remembered how Eliot had suddenly and inexplicably ordered Willmouse to bed when Willmouse had done nothing to deserve it. But . . . and I remembered. Willmouse had been talking . . . about the motor bike. I almost said it and clapped my hand to my mouth.

That must have been noticeable for they all saw it.

"What now?" groaned Madame Corbet. "Truly, these children!"

I had to pretend it was toothache. "She looks pale," said Monsieur le Directeur wearily. "Open your mouth." He looked along my teeth. "She had better go and see Dupont," he said to Madame Corbet. "These"—and he tapped two teeth—"look to me as if they should come out."

As the day went on it grew heavier; by "it" I mean this thing I was trying not to know. I was behaving like an ostrich with its head in the sand but every now and then the head would be pulled out; I hastily burrowed it back into the sand again.

Willmouse woke in the afternoon but he was drowsy and stupid and his voice was thick. Joss telephoned the hospital, Madame Corbet getting through for her, and Willmouse was given hot tea. He immediately fell asleep again, but he was warmer.

Joss stayed with him and Hester and I wandered out along the river. We tacitly agreed we should not go and see Mother; I could not have trusted myself near her. We avoided the cove and between us was a weight of silence. Even to Hester I could not speak of what was in me and as if she felt a barrier she did not speak either, which was remarkable for Hester, until we came out on the towing-path when, "Look," she said, "the *Marie France* is gone."

"It had to go sometime," I said. It did not seem important but there seemed a curious blankness on the river where the little barge had been.

We went in to goûter, getting it ourselves. Mauricette was leaning on Monsieur Armand, reading the paper over his shoulder. "That is why Monsieur Dufour came asking about Monsieur Eliot," she said in French, but I was beginning not to notice whether people spoke in French or English. I had been cutting a piece from a baguette and I stopped with the bread in my hand. "Why?" I asked . . ."

"'Vol de diamants, à Paris,'" read out Monsieur Armand. "'Coup de main audacieux dans le quartier de l'Etoile. Le mailfaiteur s'enfuit avec cent millions de francs de diamants.'"

"Diamonds?" I asked and, "What does it mean?" asked Hester.

"Only that there has been a robbery," I said.

"Tell her," said Monsieur Armand, giving the paper to me to do my translation. "Now, nicely, for your sister."

Painfully I began. "'An armed—' Qu'est-ce que c'est 'mal-faiteur'?" I asked Monsieur Armand.

"Gangster," said Monsieur Armand, who went to the cinema.

"'Armed gangster steals one hundred . . . million'—it *is* million?" I asked.

"Million," confirmed Monsieur Armand.

"'One hundred million francs' worth of jewels and escapes.

"'Once a month Mademoiselle Yvonne Lebègue, secretary to Monsieur Roger Dixonne, a diamond . . . merchant,'" I read, stumbling over the unfamiliar words, "'whose offices are in the Rue La Fayette, ninth ar—' What is that?"

"Neuvième arrondissement," explained Monsieur Armand, which left me none the wiser.

"'Collects pierres précieuses . . . precious stones, chiefly diamonds, from a colleague in the Place du Trocadéro. On Friday, towards three fifteen, Mademoiselle Lebègue was being driven on her way to the Rue La Fayette through the Rue Dumont d'Urville by Jean Sagan, Monsieur Dixonne's chauffeur. She had with her . . . un lot spécial . . . special lot of—' Qu'est-ce que c'est 'pierres taillées'?" Mauricette pretended to cut sharply with a knife. "Oh, cut stones! '. . . valued at about one hundred million francs in a small—' Qu'est-ce que c'est 'une mallette d'aluminium'?"

Mauricette seized a saucepan and tapped it to show me. "Oh, aluminium case." I had not known cases could be of aluminium. "'. . . which she placed under her feet in the car, a large Mercèdes. When the Mercèdes was almost . . . à la hauteur de la rue . . . at the top of the street near the P.T.T., a small light blue car, parked on the right side of the road, drew out suddenly and stopped . . .' in a cross? Oh, crosswise! 'across the road, forcing the Mercèdes to stop. At the same time a man appeared by the car, swung open the door by Mademoiselle Lebègue, seized the case, slammed the door, and was gone. It was so quickly and quietly done that the chauffeur did not see him at all and, though there were many people on the pavement, no one realized what had happened until Monsieur Sagan jumped out . . . aux cris de "Arrètez cet homme! Arrètez-le!" . . . crying "Stop that man! Stop him!" and they heard Mademoiselle Lebègue's cries. Meanwhile the small car had driven off. Monsieur Sagan ran through the crowd but there was no sign of the thief, who must have . . . very well known'"—I translated literally—"'known Monsieur Dixonne's habits to be able to organize this attack in less than two minutes.'"

"Ah ça! Par exemple!" cried Monsieur Armand, full of admiration. "C'est un peu fort!" He added wisely, "La femme était dans l'coup."

"What woman was in it?"

"La secrétaire," said Monsieur Armand and nodded.

Mauricette said they would catch the thief, the police had the number of the small car. Monsieur Armand said the driver was probably just an accomplice and the car was surely stolen; they would find it presently. "On verra bien, you will see," he said and I went on reading. "'This is the third time there has been one of these . . .'" I stumbled.

"Hold-ups," said Monsieur Armand.

"'. . . in this quarter. Paris police are looking for a man of thirty-five or thereabouts, tall, slim, dressed in thin trousers and a green jacket. The swiftness and . . . au . . . audacity lead them to think it is the work of an experienced thief, perhaps the international bandit Alen, who was behind the jewel raids in Cannes last year, whom all efforts by the police failed to catch.'" I read on. "What is 'une grande enquête'?" I asked.

"Cherchant partout," said Mauricette.

"Oh! Searching everywhere," and Mauricette said, "Même Monsieur Eliot." She laughed as she said it but I did not laugh. Searching everywhere. Even for Eliot! My mind seemed to give a sharp click.

The newspaper said they were checking all foreign people within a certain radius of Paris and Mauricette was teasing us. "Vous deux, Mademoiselle Cecil et Mademoiselle Hester, et ma p'tite Vicky, ma p'tite reine," and she picked up Vicky and danced with her. Then she stopped and pointed out a picture in the newspaper to me.

We were in the kitchen where everything was familiar, Monsieur Armand, Mauricette, the pots and pans; even the flies crawling on Monsieur Armand's forehead seemed friendly, almost dear; but now everything seemed to slide together into a blur behind the picture of a man and I spelled out the headline above it: "'I have seen him and shall know him again,' says Inspector Jules Cailleux of the Sûreté Générale, who is handling the case. "This time we shall get him.'"

I took the newspaper, up to Joss. "Inspector Cailleux? He was the one at Dormans," said Joss.

"Yes, on that day . . ." I broke off. I still did not like to mention that day to Joss, but Hester said, "When Eliot was queer."

There was a silence. Then I brought out huskily, "Perhaps he was queer because he did not want Inspector Cailleux to see him."

"Don't imagine things," said Joss sharply but the sharpness told me she was imagining too.

"Willmouse, wake *up*. Wake *up*! *Willmouse!*"

It was next morning. Late the night before Willmouse had stirred, smiled, and waked again. Madame Corbet must have been worried because she came straight up to him and he had had hot soup, some bread and butter, had smiled at us and gone back to sleep. In the night I had heard him rustling. He wanted to go to the Hole and I had taken him. Surely now he must be awake enough to talk . . . or not to talk, I thought desperately.

All night I had pondered, conning over these difficult bits and pieces. Why I? I thought, why should it be I? People are not sent what they cannot bear; Mother had said that in the train but that was about pain. I could have borne a pain, but this, this horrible knowledge that was in me I could not bear. It's imagination, I said, pushing it out of sight. At all costs, I thought, that was what I must do, refuse it, keep it down, be silent, not talk, not let Hester talk, or anyone else. "Willmouse, wake *up!*"

He opened his eyes. "Have I been asleep?" asked Willmouse.

"Can you understand me?" I said.

"Why not?" He was astonished.

"I want you to promise me something. My tone must have been very solemn for his eyes were as big as an owl's as he looked at me.

"Is it important?"

"Very important. Willmouse, if they—anyone—ask you if you saw anything, say nothing. Promise."

"Did I see anything?" he asked.

Two parties were coming for lunch. "You must tidy your room," Madame Corbet told me.

"Shall I make the bloodstain for you as Paul isn't here?" I asked. I had meant to be sarcastic, to show Madame Corbet we knew what frauds they were, but she only nodded. To her it was normal hotel business and she said, "You could bury the skull as well, but first put Rita and Rex in the kennel or they will dig it up now."

"Where are Rita and Rex?"

They were not on the house-step in their usual place, nor inside the house, nor in the garden; then I heard barks from the orchard, barking and whining. I remember that as I went to see what had excited them I passed the box hedge, rubbing a leaf in my hands to catch the hot bruised smell, and dawdled in the orchard to see if any greengages were left. There were a few, on the trees, overripe in the sun but still firm under the leaves; I ate both kinds and they added to the chaotic feeling in my stomach. Then, with the dog leashes in my hand, I went down the first long alley.

At the end of the alley there was a pit under the wall; it was filled with loose earth and rotting leaves, grass mowings and weeds; everything was thrown there to make a compost heap for Robert's beloved bedding plants in the top garden.

In this heap Rita was digging; her excited whines and barks sent quivers through Rex, who was sitting upright on the grass, his ears pricked. He was holding something in his mouth and his tail thumped proudly at the sight of me; though Rita found it, it was always Rex who brought the skull and he got up now and came to me and put the thing into my hand.

It was an espadrille, grey-white and sodden, with the tapes still knotted. I flinched and dropped it on the ground while Rex looked up at my face and thumped his tail.

"Wait, boy," I said. It was a sound like a croak and I took three steps to see what it was that Rita was digging.

In the brown-yellow of the leaves was something pale. I took another step and the whole orchard seemed to tilt and run into a blur as the kitchen had done when I saw Inspector Cailleux's picture, but now the orchard ran into the sky. The pale thing was a foot; a foot and ankle lying downwards, the rest was under the leaves. There was an edge of blue cotton trouser but the ankle was bare; its skin looked white and tender as the back of Vicky's neck, a young skin. There was a leaf stuck to it, a little bright yellow leaf; not knowing what I was doing, I bent down to take it off.

It was stuck; almost absently I scraped it with my nail and my finger touched the skin, and it was cold.

I had been cold for two days but this cold was different; it was a chill all its own, shivers went over me and my lips began to shake. The foot was cold and stiff with a dreadful stiffness. The smell of decay that rose up from the leaves and rotting weeds filled my mouth and nose and seemed to me the smell of death. There was no escape now. My head had come out of the sand and I had to know. The foot had worn the espadrille, Paul's espadrille . . . and this was Paul.

CHAPTER XVI

Greengage indigestion!" said Madame Corbet.

She had come upon me sick on the garden path. "Too many greengages," she said and her topknot shook not with pity but with indignation.

I did not contradict her. I could not, I could only gasp and moan; and she was right, it was as if I were trying to fling out Paul, Eliot, Les Oeillets, all of it, a sudden rising of my stomach to my mouth in the same way that the orchard had run up into the sky.

"Too big a girl to eat so many," scolded Madame Corbet.

"I'm not big. I'm little, too little," I wanted to cry but I could not speak; she had to help me, unwilling as she was, until at last I could lean against her and get my breath. "Are . . . Rita and Rex shut up?"

"I put them in the kennel," said Madame Corbet, annoyed. "I even have to do that. I have everything to see to. Everything! Have you finished?" she asked sharply.

"I—I think so."

"Then go and lie down. You will not have any lunch."

Thankfully I escaped and went upstairs. In our room I went to the washing-stand, which had not been emptied and cleaned. If it had, we were not allowed to touch it until the visitors were gone. I washed and washed my hands; I think I was trying to wash away the feeling of that-cold and the smell of the dead leaves. I remember I was trembling and the beating was back in my head. "You know what you have seen," said that beating. "You know. There is no shadow of doubt. You will have to do something now. What are you going to do?" I should have liked to creep into the unmade bed and pull the clothes over my head but Toinette was at the door. I escaped from her and went into Vicky and Hester's room.

Toinette had finished in here, it was tidy and clean; Nebuchadnezzar, getting very withered now, was in his basket on a chair by Vicky's side of the bed; there were fresh flowers, pimpernels, daisies, and wild geranium, in Hester's liqueur glass. As I noticed it I had an overwhelming desire to look at Eliot— Eliot who had done . . . that. I opened the drawer where she hid her photograph from Toinette. The little frame was lying on its face. I picked it up, and it was empty.

I was still staring at the empty frame when Joss came in. "Madame Corbet says—" she broke off. Then, "I took it," said Joss.

"The photograph?" She nodded. "So that they shouldn't . . ." I do not know why I asked her that. She could not know who "they" were but as if she did know she shook her head. "I told Hester I wanted to copy it—make a portrait." Her face was so set and hard it looked like a stone carving of Joss. "But you didn't,"

I said and asked, "What did you do with it?" She did not answer and I said, "You gave it to Monsieur Dufour."

"No."

"Then what?"

"I sent it to Inspector Cailleux."

"The Dormans man?"

"Yes."

"Joss!"

"Eliot shouldn't play fast and loose." She was not stone now. "That is what they call it and that is what it is; keep you, then push you away, take you and push you away. It's cruel. It's not only me; he has done it to Mademoiselle Zizi, and Monsieur Armand says the diamond merchant's secretary woman as well. He played with us, like—like chess, she and Mademoiselle Zizi and me."

"He wasn't playing with you."

"Shut up," blazed Joss. "Shut up!" but I was steady.

"He didn't play with any of us," I said. "We were the only people he didn't play with."

Joss went to the window and stood with her back to me.

"When did you do it?" I asked.

"Yesterday. As soon as I knew, after you had brought me the paper, I wrote and went down to the office and asked for a stamp. Madame Corbet gave it to me. I went out to the corner and posted it. It caught the post."

"You don't know it was he."

"If it isn't they won't come," said Joss but we were both waiting for them to come. "I knew it as soon as I saw the paper," said Joss.

"Just from Inspector Cailleux?" I said, marvelling.

"Not from him. From Eliot." And she cried, "That was what made him so unhappy."

"They will get it this morning," I said slowly.

"And Paris isn't very far," said Joss.

There was a silence. We were both listening. Then, "What will they do to him, Cecil?" asked Joss. "Will they put him in prison?"

"They have to catch him first." That was ripped out of me, a hope. Then I knew that I ought not to hope. I said, "Joss . . ."

She had sat down on the bed; she was still listening for sounds outside and, almost absent-mindedly, she raised her eyes to me. "They won't put him in prison," I said.

Her eyes came alive. She rapped out, "Why not?"

"Because if they catch him I think he will have to be hanged." Holding to the bedpost, I told her what I had found. When I began she put out her hand and caught my wrist as if she would stop me, it was a stranglehold and my hand went limp and white; when I had finished and she let me go the blood rushing back into it hurt excruciatingly. There was another silence, then, "They don't hang people in France," she said. "They guillotine them."

"It's the visitors for lunch." I said that quickly when we heard the car slow at the gates.

"It's too early," said Joss.

We were in her room and had only to go to the window to see what car it was, but we stayed huddled together on the bed. The car drove in and stopped. Joss laid her cold hand on my cold one. "Cecil, you look."

"I can't."

"You can. You didn't send for them."

I did not go to the window but went downstairs just as Monsieur Dufour walked in. "What, again?" said Madame Corbet, who was crossing the hall.

"Again," said Monsieur Dufour; his voice did not sound kind but curt and angry. Behind him were two other men; one was big, in a tweed jacket, and carried a dispatch case; the other was small, and I held to the banisters as I recognized him. Yes, it was the Dormans man with the sandy hair and moustache, even the sand-and-olive-coloured suit; he had been in the newspaper, now he was here. Inspector Cailleux had come. A curious little sound came from me and seemed to float out into the hall.

As Monsieur Dufour talked rapidly and angrily to Madame Corbet she caught sight of me. "Go into the garden and call Mademoiselle Zizi," she rapped out in French.

Mademoiselle Zizi must have been lying in the long chair on the terrace but I think she too had heard the car because as I came to her she was standing and as still as Joss had been. Did she have some sixth-sense warning? I reached her and she gripped me. "Who is it?"

"The police."

"Police!" Her face looked suddenly older but her eyes were like a child's, filled with fear, looking far over my head.

"Where is Irène?"

"With them. They want you." I paused. "Mademoiselle Zizi . . ."

No answer, only the fingers gripping me, kneading my arm.

"Mademoiselle Zizi." I said it more loudly. Her eyes came back to me but they looked quite senseless. With my free hand I gave her fingers a sharp slap but she did not seem to feel it.

"Zizi!" Madame Corbet came down the terrace. "Zizi. Vas-y."

Then Mademoiselle Zizi did let me go. She looked at Madame Corbet and backed away from her. "You!" she said, her voice ugly. "You sent for them."

"I? Why should I?" Madame Corbet put out her hands but Mademoiselle Zizi still backed away from her.

"It was you."

"Zizi. Qu'est-ce que tu nous racontes?"

"It was you."

"Hush," I said like a grown-up. "Listen. *Listen!*" and I stamped my foot. They stared. "There is something you should see before you go in. It—he—" I thought I was going to be sick again and tumbled the words out. "It's in the orchard."

"What 'it'?" but I could not tell them.

"Look, quickly, in the heap where the leaves are thrown."

"Et maintenant qu'est-ce que tu nous racontes?"

"Quickly."

"What *is* it?" but I had taken refuge in being a child and had begun to cry. "Something . . . I think . . . I found. Oh look! Look quickly. I will go in and say you are coming, but go. Go."

The policemen were in the bar, where Mauricette was bringing them drinks on a tray. Monsieur Dufour was walking up and down, looking miserable and angry, the other two were sitting calmly at a table; Inspector Cailleux was looking round him with what I imagined was a detective look, taking every detail in. I could see Joss on the stairs, her hand holding the rail.

"Et Mademoiselle de Presle? Elle vient?" barked Monsieur Dufour at me.

With Joss watching I was dignified in spite of my red eyes. "Dans un petit moment," I said, closing the garden door behind me; but Monsieur Dufour sprang forward and wrenched it open for, just then, down in the orchard Mademoiselle Zizi began to scream.

CHAPTER XVII

W hen anything happens in a house the children are treated like cattle. We were rounded up, herded upstairs and into our rooms; as we went up we could hear Mademoiselle Zizi having hysterics, and Monsieur Dufour trying to calm her. Madame Corbet had to leave her to him, for as usual she had everything to do: control Mauricette, Toinette, and Nicole, who seemed to want to have hysterics too, enlist Monsieur Armand's help, telephone the doctor, install Inspector Cailleux in the little salon, and allow his assistant to use the telephone in the office. I have always wondered what happened to the parties for lunch.

After Mademoiselle Zizi stopped screaming a horrible calm lay over the house, the house not the garden; the garden was full of police and Rita and Rex bayed frantically in the kennel. Each time their noise rose it meant a fresh batch of police had arrived. Monsieur Armand saw us looking out of the windows and came up and shuttered them. "Better not to look," he said gently but we could not help looking through the cracks, all except Joss, who sat as if she had been frozen on the bed.

A dark blue van drove up.

"What's that?" asked Willmouse fearfully.

"I expect it's some stores for the kitchen," I said, trying to soothe him, "only some stores."

"It's the dead car," said Vicky, who was not supposed to know anything. "It has come for Paul."

The truth spoken so flatly shocked us and we stayed perfectly still listening to the tramp of feet. "He's on a stretcher," said Vicky, peering, "all covered up."

I had a hiccup that shook me from my heels, to my head. Hester began to cry. "Paul saved up for his lorry," she said. "Why? Why did God do it?"

"God didn't," said Vicky. "It was Eliot. Monsieur Armand said so."

"It was all my fault," said Joss. Sitting on the bed, she twisted her hands together. "If I had gone on painting. Cecil told me to but I would go to the party."

"We went to the party too," said Hester loyally.

"If I hadn't smiled at him . . ."

"Well, if we had never talked to him . . ." I could say that.

". . . he would never have come up the ladder," said Joss, not listening.

"Did he come up a ladder?" Hester and the Littles asked. "Why?" they asked, round-eyed.

"To . . . look at Joss."

"Why?"

"Men do at women," said Willmouse.

I told them how Eliot came. "He needn't have come. It was

because he thought we were in trouble. He could have gone," I said. "He shook the ladder and Paul fell."

"Nobody meant it, it happened," said Hester; she added mournfully, "And now Eliot has gone."

"I saw him go." They all turned to me, listening carefully as I told them.

"That was how he was dressed," said Willmouse, nodding, when I described the clothes. "But . . . I can't believe it," said Willmouse. He looked stunned.

"I can," said Hester, and feeling our surprise she explained, "Eliot always said, 'I'm sorry. I had to do that.' If you are all right really, really all right, you don't do things that are sorry."

Presently Madame Corbet appeared. "He wants to see you."

"Who?"

"Inspector Cailleux."

"In our scarecrows?"

"It doesn't matter," said Madame Corbet as one who says, "Nothing matters now."

She drove us downstairs, all except Joss, who was not to be ordered. "I shall come when I'm ready," she said.

Inspector Cailleux was in the little salon. We had never been allowed to enter it, now we were to go in, in our scarecrows, and sit on the yellow satin chairs but, first, we had to wait. The door was open; we could see Monsieur Dufour and the tweed-coated man. When we peeped round we saw that Inspector Cailleux, in his funny-coloured suit, was sitting at the pretty centre table with its painting of cupids and ribbons; it seemed terrible it should be used for this. Another man was at a table carried in from the bar and put in the window.

He was writing but the other three were talking; by straining every sense I could just keep up.

"I can*not* believe it," Monsieur Dufour was saying. He was walking up and down. "Everyone knew Monsieur Eliot. Why, he was here, dining at this big dinner with us all last night. He must have a nerve of iron."

"He has," said the clipped, soft voice of Inspector Cailleux.

"What does he say?" whispered Willmouse.

They must have heard Willmouse whisper, for Inspector Cailleux asked, "Can those children understand French?"

"Very little," said Monsieur Dufour, "except the big one perhaps." He came to the door and glanced at us. "She is not here yet," and he asked, "Shall I close the door?"

"No, leave it. It's too hot," said Inspector Cailleux.

The talk went on. "But how?" Monsieur Dufour was saying. "How? Monsieur Eliot was here all afternoon. You have heard."

"I have heard. That does not mean to say he was."

"But he was. We have evidence. Here all afternoon. Then how was he in Paris, in the Rue Dumont d'Urville, at three o'clock? If this was his work he had an accomplice."

"He had no accomplice." Inspector Cailleux's voice sounded tired. "He works alone or practically alone; there may be a man hired to drive a car or to telephone, but then he is discarded. We have caught them, Dufour, and they know nothing. Often they don't know who he is. He's too clever to have accomplices; sooner or later one of them would give him away. No, never accomplices, only tools, simple people; especially women."

"Especially women." I knew Monsieur Dufour was thinking of Mademoiselle Zizi; I was thinking of the simple people, of us.

"But how? How?" said Monsieur Dufour again. "I don't understand."

"If we could understand; it would not be Allen."

"What are they talking about?" asked Willmouse, and I lost the rest until Inspector Cailleux said slowly, "I know that man's work as if it were my own."

"Tell us," Willmouse commanded me urgently and I translated sentence by sentence as best I could, but it was hard work listening and telling.

"But . . . right under our noses!" said Monsieur Dufour.

"Under your noses," said Inspector Cailleux. Then he threw down his pen. "What's the good? He has had thirty-six hours. He is hundreds of miles away by now."

"I don't think he is," said Willmouse when I had translated.

"What do you mean?"

"I know where Eliot is."

"Where?"

"On the barge," said Willmouse, "the *Marie France*." The *Marie France* had gone and I remembered that soft strange hoot in the night.

I gazed at my little brother. "But how did you know?"

"He was dressed for it," said Willmouse simply. He added, "Barges go very slowly but I don't suppose they will think of looking for him there."

"Cecil!" said Hester urgently.

I looked up. Mademoiselle Zizi had come into the bar. I had seen her once without her make-up but now her face seemed to have come through it. She was a strange grey-white colour and her face was knotted as if it had cords in it and her hair was tumbled half down on her shoulders. She looked at us, then into the little salon and pointed to it inquiringly and then at us again.

We shook our heads.

Her eyes turned from one to another of us; they seemed to be asking us, and she put her fingers to her lips. Slowly, solemnly, we nodded.

Madame Corbet's quick voice was heard in the hall and Mademoiselle Zizi turned almost in a panic to go. In the doorway she met Joss.

Joss stopped when she saw Mademoiselle Zizi. For a moment they faced each other. Then Mademoiselle Zizi spoke.

"They have told me. So! It was you who sent the photograph."

"Of course." Joss crossed in front of her and said, "Let me sit down, Hester."

In the little salon the voices grew louder. We listened and I said, "They're talking about us."

"We have seen everyone now," Monsieur Dufour had said.

"Except the children." That was Inspector Cailleux.

"They cannot be very important. At least, only the big girl."

"They may be very important. Call them in. I shall take the small ones first and remember," ordered Inspector Cailleux, "don't speak to the big one. Ignore her."

"It will make her nervous."

"I want her nervous," said Inspector Cailleux.

Monsieur Dufour came to the salon door and beckoned us in. He started when he saw Mademoiselle Zizi. "Zizi," he said, "you should be resting."

"Resting!"

"Well, something. Don't stay here. Please," and he said, "Irène. Take her." Madame Corbet put her arm round Mademoiselle Zizi and led her away as we filed in.

"Asseyez-vous, mes enfants."

Because we knew our scarecrows were very dirty we sat on the edges of the yellow chairs. Last of all Joss, her chin high, spots of red in her cheeks, took a chair by the door.

"Must the little children be in this?" asked Monsieur Dufour in French.

Inspector Cailleux did not raise his head. "They are in it," he said.

He wrote for a few minutes, then suddenly he sat up and looked at us, one after the other. I felt myself go hot, then cold. I think we all had blanched faces. Hester looked like . . . like a peeled nut, I thought; as for Joss, it seemed she had put on her mask painted with those two bright spots.

"Which of you took this photograph?"

It was said so casually, and in English, that we started. I do not know what we had expected; to be bullied, asked our names and ages, or have our thumbs twisted, but he was simply holding the snapshot up.

"I did," said Hester with modest pleasure.

"And you are . . ." He looked at a paper. "Hester?" She nodded. "Ten years old?" Hester's curls bobbed again. "Ten years old," said Inspector Cailleux in French to Monsieur Dufour, "and she has succeeded in doing what no one else has ever done, getting a photograph of Allen." Then in English, "I must congratulate you, ma p'tite. It is most valuable."

"Valuable?" The pleasure was wiped from Hester's face. "You mean . . . my photograph helped you?"

"Helped me! It brought me straight here." And to Monsieur Dufour again he said, "I am one of the few, the very few, who have seen Allen. I had him once—for an hour."

"He got away?" Monsieur Dufour sounded almost pleased.

"He got away." Inspector Cailleux's voice forbade any more questions and I remembered how the newspaper had said: ". . . whom the police failed to catch."

"I must ask you for the negative"—Inspector Cailleux was speaking to Hester again—"but we shall give you something very pretty in exchange. A doll. You would like a doll?"

"No," said Hester, her eyes horrified.

"Eliot gave me a doll," said Vicky. "We don't want yours."

"Listen," said Inspector Cailleux, "I am going to speak to you as if you were not children but grown up. You know this man Allen?"

We shook our heads.

"You know Monsieur Eliot?"

We nodded. "He is our friend," said Willmouse.

"Your friend is a thief," said Inspector Cailleux. Hester and the Littles were listening to him solemnly and he warmed. "A thief who stole in many countries, deceived people, took their money, and was often cruel to them. I must tell you that sometimes he killed them."

"Like he did Paul?" asked Vicky, interested.

"Vicky, you are not to say things like that," Joss cut in from where she sat by the door.

"If you please, Mademoiselle . . ." said Inspector Cailleux.

"But—" began Joss hotly.

"I must ask you to be quiet. I shall come to you . . . later."

He made that sound so frightening that I had to press myself down on my chair not to gasp.

Inspector Cailleux returned to the Littles. "He killed Paul," he said. "Are you going to like him after that?"

Hester, Willmouse, and Vicky said instantly, "Yes."

Inspector Cailleux looked nonplussed and perhaps a little angry. When he spoke again his voice was sharp. "Like him or not, you have a duty. You know what duty is?"

We all nodded. Eliot was our friend—but when a friend kills a friend? And with a paper knife. I felt sure now it was the paper knife, or what we had thought was a paper knife. A rift was being torn between us and Eliot; each word that Inspector Cailleux said made that rift more.

"If you know anything, have seen anything strange or out of place, about this man Allen or Eliot," he was saying, "it is your duty to tell me."

Dead silence.

"Your duty," said Inspector Cailleux and his eyes went over each of us again. I dared not put my hands down on my chair in case they left marks as they had left them on the window sill.

Hester was the most honest of us and the most easily worked upon. I had guessed she would feel she had to say something and in the silence she put up her hand.

"Well?"

"He . . ." said Hester as if her throat were dry. "He . . ."

"Yes?" said Inspector Cailleux encouragingly. "He?"

"He lay in the cove . . ." said Hester.

"Yes?" said Inspector Cailleux again, but I had pinched her and she shut her lips.

Again there was silence but this, of course, could not go on; they were the police. I thought Inspector Cailleux had seen that pinch; detectives saw everything or they would not be detectives. He was looking at me without appearing to look and it was borne in on me afresh that I was the only one who knew . . . everything, I thought. I could not help another little gasp and this time his eyes looked straight at me for a second. They looked away at once but I knew I was marked; quite rightly, not even Joss, who had been so quick to guess, knew all the pieces that fitted together. Each of them knew something but I knew it all. What was I to do? Here in front of Inspector Cailleux all dreams and wishes fled. These were the police. Soon I should have to tell.

It was beginning to come out.

"You were the one who had the sleeping dose." Inspector Cailleux had turned to Willmouse and he asked Monsieur Dufour, "You think Allen gave the dose to him?"

"The chef, Monsieur Armand, says Monsieur . . . Allen took up a tray for the boy. We think, but we do not know."

"We can guess," said Inspector Cailleux, and to Willmouse, "What was on the tray you were brought?"

"Food," said Willmouse. "Banquet food; chicken and party toast and a meringue. A beautiful meringue," said Willmouse remembering.

"Anything to drink?"

"Grenadine."

"The supper things were washed up," said Monsieur Dufour, "so that, of course, we do not absolutely know."

"We can guess," said Inspector Cailleux again and his pale eyes studied Willmouse. "This child knew something."

"What could a child of his age know?"

Inspector Cailleux shrugged. "Children are everywhere, like insects. They can know anything."

"Hm," said Monsieur Dufour thoughtfully. "They say he slept for two days. It must have been strong."

"The drug or the reason?"

"Both," said Monsieur Dufour. "But it was abominable! To drug a child."

"This was Allen," Inspector Cailleux reminded him. "The little boy is lucky to be alive."

"*Who* are they talking about?" Willmouse whispered more urgently to me.

"You."

"Why?"

"Because they think . . . Eliot . . . put you to sleep."

"*Eliot?*"

"Yes."

"Why? Why?" said Willmouse imperiously to Inspector Cailleux.

"Because, my little man, you knew something he did not want you to tell. It was not a very pleasant thing to do to you, was it?"

"It was silly," said Willmouse. He was wounded. "Why didn't he ask me not to tell? He needn't have put me to sleep. He could have *trusted* me."

"Was this man God to them?" asked Inspector Cailleux. He was getting angry and the questions came fast.

"Why did he send you to bed?"

"I was out late."

"Why were you out late?"

"I had been for my walk."

"Where did you go?"

"Along the river."

"Did you see anything?"

They were coming closer . . . like bloodhounds, I thought, and prickled with apprehension. "Did you see anything?" asked Inspector Cailleux peremptorily.

"I saw the barge," said Willmouse.

"What barge?"

"The *Marie France*."

"What was the barge doing?"

"Nothing," said Willmouse truthfully but Inspector Cailleux was looking deeply into him.

"Do you like barges?" he asked.

"No."

"Then there was something especial about this one? Something you saw perhaps? Perhaps?" rapped Inspector Cailleux.

"I would rather not talk to you," said Willmouse.

"I am not *playing*," cried Inspector Cailleux and hit the little table with his fist so that it shook. Vicky burst into tears.

"I don't like it," she wailed. "I want Mother."

As if Mother's name had been a touchstone we all began to weep, except Joss who was still disassociated from us; I was ashamed but the tears were gathering, unbearably heavy and hot in my eyes. Mother. If only Mother were here for us in this terror! But there was no one, no one for us and we quailed like little rabbits, chased and cornered, ready to be snared. Helplessly we wept. There was more to come, more shockingness, but we had moved Monsieur Dufour. He protested, "I told you this was not for children."

"Some of them are not children."

We jumped. Mademoiselle Zizi was standing in the doorway. At the sight of her distorted face even Vicky was quelled.

"You are asking them questions," said Mademoiselle Zizi. "Why? You need only ask her." She pointed at Joss. "Ask her what the ladder was doing on the lawn under her window, why the marks of it were on the grass." Madame Corbet had come running after Mademoiselle Zizi but Mademoiselle Zizi shook her off. "Ask her."

Inspector Cailleux looked at Joss, who had risen like a girl in class. Slowly I rose too but no one noticed me.

"Is that a child?" said Mademoiselle Zizi, and to Monsieur Dufour, "You have seen her with your own eyes, how she behaved at the dinner. She drove Paul out of his mind. You saw that too. Well, ask her what happened. The ladder was at her window. Elle a couché avec l'un après l'autre?"

I did not understand the word "sleep" used like that, "sleep with one after the other," nor its import; I was only sure that in some way it was hideous and unjust and I moved nearer to Joss. "She didn't sleep," I said. "She was wide awake. Why, she came to my room and sent me in—"

"*You*?" Their eyes all shifted to me.

"Tiens! They begin young in England," said Mademoiselle Zizi.

"Don't be a fool," said Joss curtly to me.

"These little children must go *out*," said Monsieur Dufour, springing up distressed, but Hester and the Littles had already left their yellow satin chairs and come to Joss and me; they did not understand what the talk was about but knew we were threatened and they stood loyally round us.

Once again we seemed small and alone in that French house. Monsieur Dufour was kindly but he was thinking of Mademoiselle Zizi. Only one person would have defended us, Eliot . . . and he . . . I could not go on. I swallowed, and felt as if the tears were running down my throat.

"So! Two of you," said Mademoiselle Zizi. "And this is what I took into my house."

Your dear house! In that moment of misery I almost said it. Les Oeillets, the gold-green days, the love, to end in this.

It was at that moment I heard a sound in the courtyard outside that made me look up. These were the windows from which Mademoiselle Zizi had so often watched for Eliot, listening for the Rolls. Now I looked out and saw the big gate was shut as it had been on our first night. It had been shut by the police. The sound I had heard was the jangling of the bell.

I do not know how I heard it in the confusion in the room but it seemed to join onto the bell of that first night; the sound belonged . . . to us? I thought, puzzled.

A gendarme opened the wicket; he spoke for a moment to someone outside and opened the gate.

Inside the salon there was turmoil. The other two policemen had jumped up and Madame Corbet was explaining to them, shouting over our heads while Monsieur Dufour talked to Mademoiselle Zizi as if he was scolding her. Only Inspector Cailleux stayed at his desk, quietly watching.

"Zizi! You haven't a shadow of proof," scolded Monsieur Dufour.

"Haven't I?" She wheeled on him. "Why did I have to put Monsieur Joubert out of the hotel?" Everyone stopped to listen. "They said it was painting!" said Mademoiselle Zizi and she spat the word again. "Painting!"

I had felt Joss quivering, but now happened something so alarming that it burned out everything else. Joss, dignified, aloof, almost grown-up Joss, crumpled like a little girl. "Mother. I want Mother," she wailed like Vicky.

We stood round her, appalled too. "Help me. Help me," sobbed Joss.

We could not help her. How could we? We barely understood. There was no one to help us now and soon, soon I should have to . . . Helpless in my tears I looked out of the window and saw that a man had come in through the gate. He was dressed in a grey suit and brown felt hat and was followed by a porter with a handcart and two leather suitcases. There was something very familiar about the man; his small figure looked square and solid in the Frenchness of the courtyard, his skin fresh and pink beside the dark, sallow-skinned gendarme and porter, and there was a wonderful calmness about him. My heart suddenly calmed too. It was Uncle William.

"Uncle William!" The shout I gave filled the little salon. I do not know how we burst out of it, past Mademoiselle Zizi, Madame Corbet, and Monsieur Dufour. I think I heard Inspector Cailleux ordering us to sit down but I was not listening, nor were the others. All of us, even Joss, rushed through the bar into the hall.

Uncle William came in. Joss threw herself into his arms, I had mine round his neck, Vicky and Hester were hugging his legs, Willmouse danced up and down in front of him. Uncle William! Dear, dear, dear Uncle William!

CHAPTER XVIII

"My name is Bullock."

We had always winced and thought that people must laugh when Uncle William said that but now nobody laughed, nor did we wince. We kept close behind him, Hester even had a corner of his coat clutched in her hand. "Bullock"—and he put down his card on the desk—"of Bullock, Roper and Twiss, Solicitors, Southstone. That is in Sussex, England."

"A votre service, Monsieur," said Inspector Cailleux and introduced the others. "Monsieur Dufour, Monsieur Lemaître, Monsieur Aubry." They bowed. "Madame Corbet," said Inspector Cailleux; he did not introduce Mademoiselle Zizi.

"You have some trouble?" asked Uncle William after he had shaken hands. "The police. . . ?"

"You have doubtless heard at the station or on your way here of these shocking events," said Inspector Cailleux dryly.

"I have heard nothing. I do not speak French," said Uncle William. His calm, flat English voice sounded wonderfully unexcited. "I have come to take my sister—if she can travel—and my nieces and nephew home—to England," he added firmly, looking at us.

"You said you wouldn't come and you came!" said Hester, stroking his coat.

"How did you know to come now, just now!" cried Joss, still clinging to him.

"But I was sent for," said Uncle William.

"Sent for?"

Freeing himself from us, he said, "This came yesterday," and from his wallet took out a piece of paper and unfolded it; it was a telegram. He read aloud, "COME IMMEDIATELY HOTEL DES OEILLETS VIEUX-MOUTIERS MARNE FRANCE YOUR SISTER IN HOSPITAL CHILDREN URGENTLY—REPEAT URGENTLY—NEED YOUR HELP."

"But who sent it?" asked Madame Corbet.

"It isn't signed," said Uncle William.

"Someone must have sent it," said Inspector Cailleux and looked round on us all. I tried to put a surreptitious hand on Hester but I was too late.

"Eliot, of course," said Hester.

"Eliot!" That came from Joss, Mademoiselle Zizi, Madame Corbet, and Inspector Cailleux.

"Yes. He *always* did look after us," said Hester, beaming.

"The fool!" Mademoiselle Zizi's cry rang out as she darted across the room and snatched the telegram from Uncle William. She was crumpling it in her hand, tearing it with her teeth as they caught her. Inspector Cailleux ripped it away and Monsieur Dufour and Madame Corbet struggled to hold her as the little sheet of paper was smoothed out and pieced together on the table.

"Châlons. Eleven twenty-five yesterday morning."

"He was heading for the German border," said Monsieur Dufour.

"Obviously," said Inspector Cailleux and snapped, "Get me Lavalle on the telephone." Then he stopped. "No, wait. Châlons," he said, puzzled. "But Châlons is almost here."

"C'est à vingt-et-un kilomètres," said the man in the window.

"Twenty-one kilometres at eleven o'clock yesterday," said Inspector Cailleux.

"He had been at the dinner," reminded Monsieur Dufour.

"But only until about midnight. He had at least nine or ten hours," said Inspector Cailleux. "I don't understand," but he said it as if in a minute, or minutes, he would understand and he began to pace up and down. Mademoiselle Zizi was quiet now, limp and sobbing against Madame Corbet.

"Could he be walking?" asked Monsieur Dufour.

"With the roads watched?"

"Cross country?"

"There are roads into Châlons," said Inspector Cailleux irritably and he walked up and down. "Somewhere slow, where we would not look for him. Of course not. We are looking everywhere fast. Very clever, Monsieur Allen. Slow. Vieux-Moutiers, Châlons, into Germany."

"Châlons? You mean Châlons-sur-Marne?" said Uncle William in his pleasant voice. "On the Marne?"

"The Marne!" Inspector Cailleux stopped. "The Marne!"

From the river, into our silence, came the hoot of a passing barge.

ABOUT THE AUTHOR

Rumer Godden (1907–1998) was the acclaimed author of over sixty works of fiction and nonfiction for adults and children. Born in England, she and her siblings grew up in Narayanganj, India, and she later spent many years living in Calcutta and Kashmir. Nine of her novels were made into films, including *Black Narcissus*; *The Greengage Summer*; and *The River*, which was filmed by Jean Renoir. Godden won the Whitbread Literary Award for children's literature in 1972, and in 1993 she was named an Officer of the Most Excellent Order of the British Empire. She died at the age of ninety in Dumfriesshire, UK.

RUMER GODDEN

FROM OPEN ROAD MEDIA

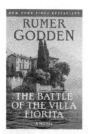

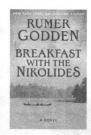

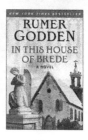

OPEN ROAD

INTEGRATED MEDIA

INTEGRATED MEDIA

9 781504 066587